'I've been thinking out the rota,' John said. 'You should be free on Thursday afternoon. We'll run down to the Cottage Hospital, it's quite near Land's End, they tell me. What time shall I pick you up?'

How late can I say, Rebecca wondered, not relishing spending a long afternoon in his company. 'Can we discuss things later?' Her voice was almost pleading.

'No need,' John said brusquely. 'It's all settled. Three o'clock.' He studied her untouched food. 'You haven't eaten a thing . . . do I disturb you that much, Rebecca? Why—do you know?'

Kathleen Farrell had an Irish father and a Scottish mother. She was born in South Africa, but they settled in England while she was still a child. After six years working in a Threadneedle Street bank, Kathleen Farrell volunteered for the WAAFS and worked on Britain's then highly secret radar defence system. She married into the RAF and while bringing up four sons and a daughter worked as a free-lance journalist. She now writes Medical Romances as her daughter is a hospital surgeon and enjoys helping her with the medical background on her stories.

A STORMY PARTNERSHIP

BY

KATHLEEN FARRELL

MILLS & BOON LIMITED
ETON HOUSE   18-24 PARADISE ROAD
RICHMOND   SURREY   TW9 1SR

*First published in Great Britain 1989
by Mills & Boon Limited*

© Kathleen Farrell 1989

*Australian copyright 1989
Philippine copyright 1989
This edition 1989*

ISBN 0 263 76512 1

*Set in Plantin 12 on 12 pt.
03–8908–43164*

Typeset in Great Britain by JCL Graphics, Bristol

Made and printed in Great Britain

CHAPTER ONE

'SHE'S bleeding, and bleeding quite profusely!' Dr Rebecca Shaw's green eyes looked from the patient to the anaesthetist standing at the head of the operating-table. 'While you're sorting out an emergency blood transfusion, please have my registrar called to come down. Tell him it looks like an ectopic pregnancy, not acute appendicitis as we'd thought.' Then, turning to the scrub sister, she said, 'I'll have to extend the incision to gain access to the fallopian tubes.' Having handed over the scalpel Sister Anne Campbell immediately connected the suction, removing the blood welling up from the pelvis. With the wound lengthened across the abdomen to the midline, Rebecca opened the rectus sheath and divided the lateral third of the rectus muscle. Accepting the two artery clips Sister Anne was holding out in readiness, she divided the inferior epigastric artery and enlarged the opening into the peritoneum.

Deftly, she reached for the fallopian tube and brought the ruptured ectopic pregnancy to the surface of the wound.

Anne, competent as usual, this time anticipated a request for two soft bowel-clamps, and passed

them over to be put across the fallopian tube and
related feeding blood-vessels on each side of the
rupture.

Rebecca gave a deep sigh of relief when able to
announce, 'The bleeding's been controlled!' She
looked around searchingly, expecting to see the
registrar watching to make sure she was doing all
that should be done. To her surprise, there was
no one present except the usual theatre staff.

'Please phone switchboard and ask what's
happened to the registrar,' she called out to one
of the nurses.

'Switchboard says the new one can't be located,
and the locum registrar has already left the
hospital,' the nurse informed her, the receiver
still to her ear. 'The difficulty seems to be that
they don't know the name of the new surgical
registrar, the new rota not having been posted up
yet. Do you know his name, Dr Shaw?'

'No, I haven't the remotest idea.' Rebecca's
reply was muffled by her mask as she bent over
the patient to remove the fallopian tube together
with the ruptured ectopic, then doubly ligate the
blood-vessels and check the opposite fallopian
tube and ovaries, before washing out any
remaining blood clot by means of warm saline
irrigation. Having only once assisted at a similar
operation, never having done one herself, she was
having to rely solely on her memory and book-
learning, so was finding it all quite a strain.

Suddenly a door opened at the back of the
theatre. 'Are you stopping the bleeding by

packing the pelvis?' asked a deep voice after a moment or two.

At the sound Rebecca's heart jumped, then began to pound. She knew that voice only too well, although it seemed deeper than she remembered. Her mouth dried, her knees shook a little, and it was only by sheer will-power that she pulled herself together to concentrate on the job in hand.

Taking the needle-holder and suture from Anne, she began the stitching, fervently hoping no one would notice the slight, uncontrollable tremor of her hands.

Fortunately Anne took it upon herself to face the stranger and speak up. 'Dr Shaw's done better than pack the pelvis,' she said proudly. 'She's removed the source of bleeding and is about to close the abdomen. She's our best junior surgeon!' Then, becoming more formal, 'Excuse me, but you haven't introduced yourself,' she reminded him. 'I'm Sister Campbell, the senior theatre sister.'

'Introductions can wait, the patient must be put first,' replied the voice Rebecca was finding so disturbing. 'Should I be needed, I'll be in the doctors' rest-room having a cup of coffee.'

Grateful for the respite, Rebecca was able to give her full attention back to the patient until the last suture was added, and the dressing securely in place over the wound.

'I feel so sorry for young Wendy,' Anne remarked as she walked to the scrubbing-room with Rebecca. 'Quite probably she didn't even know she was expecting.'

'She assured me she wasn't. She'll be worried when she wakes up and finds out what her trouble was. I don't suppose she knows anything about ectopic pregnancies—most people don't, unless they happen to know someone who's had one, or they're in the medical profession themselves.'

'Did you see the new registrar?' Anne asked as she undid the ties down the back of Rebecca's green surgical-gown.

'No, he was behind me all the time and I was too busy to to turn round.'

'Pity,' remarked Anne. 'He looked quite impressive. I like big men with strong faces. I think you'd have approved of him.'

'No doubt I won't be able to avoid seeing him from now on.' Rebecca frowned in a troubled way, causing Anne to give her a questioning glance.

'Oh, ignore me.' Rebecca half smiled reassuringly. 'I'm just tired. That operation was quite an ordeal, I'd never dealt with an ectopic pregnancy by myself before. It was a bit much not having a registrar there to give me some guidance.'

'Still, you managed OK, which is something to be proud of.' Anne gave her a congratulatory pat on the back. 'Anaesthetist Dunn seems very satisfied with Wendy's condition too, and for once he held back all his unnecessary criticisms, so what have you to worry about?'

If Anne only knew! thought Rebecca wryly, bracing herself to go to the doctors' room to write up her operation notes, fully aware that the new registrar would be awaiting her there, for she was to assist him in the next operation on the list. There was no way she could elude him any longer, so it was far better to get the reunion over, then perhaps her heart would settle down again.

With this idea in mind, she stood in the doorway, an incongruous figure in an overlarge blue and white theatre-suit, her surgical cap still on her head, her mask still in place.

There was only one person in the rest-room. Hesitantly, Rebecca entered.

'Hello, Richard,' she called diffidently to the tall, white-coated man who was looking out of the window.

He turned with an air of annoyed surprise. '*John*, if you don't mind,' he corrected her, 'not Richard.'

She gaped at him, stunned for a moment, then moved back in some alarm as he took a couple of quick strides towards her. All he did, however, was remove her surgical cap, freeing her red-gold curls to tumble down around her shoulders.

'So, it really is you, Rebecca. I thought I recognised the hair, even from what little I could see of it in theatre. I didn't expect to find you doing surgery, though.'

'Sorry to have mistaken you for someone else,' Rebecca murmured. 'The rota was only just

being put up when I left theatre and, besides being
sure your voice was that of a certain Richard Barrie,
I heard a nurse read out,"Mr Barrie" from the list,
so naturally I presumed——'

John Barrie's face had clouded over again.
'There was never anyone for you but cousin
Richard, was there?' he interrupted coldly. 'Well,
back to theatre . . .' He glanced at the pen and
green paper in her hand. 'Get busy writing up
your operation notes; I'm waiting!'

'You certainly sound like Richard,' she
commented, sitting at the coffee-table and
thinking him just as autocratic and dictatorial as
her fiancé.

He ignored her remark. 'Have you finished
writing?' he asked impatiently, after a silent
minute or two.

'For the moment.' She stood up. 'Richard's
cousin?' she said reflectively. 'I don't remember
meeting you. And tell me—why did you remove
my cap? You didn't ask my permission.'

'Merely for identification purposes,' he replied
tersely. 'Your mask hid your face, and I could see
only a strand or two of your hair. I needed to see
all of it to make sure you were you. The colour is
unique.'

'Some people call it a Caribbean sunset,' she
said with a chuckle. 'But you've got me confused,
Mr Barrie. When and where did we meet? Can
you remind me?'

'At your engagement party. You wouldn't have
noticed me—you had eyes only for Richard.' His

face expressionless, he strode along the corridor with her, then after a moment added, 'I suppose I should have asked before lifting your cap from your head, but I was rather overwhelmed at the time.'

Which was as much of an apology as he was likely to offer, thought Rebecca, going on to ask what had brought him to the Cornish hospital.

He took his time about answering, then said, 'Tiring of working overseas, I came home to see my family, heard news that made me want to stay in England, saw an advert in the *BMJ* about a vacancy here for a senior surgical registrar, so applied for the job—and got it, of course. Also had the offers of others, but Cornwall was my choice. I had my reasons.'

An arbitrary reply, decided Rebecca, which proved that John Barrie was every bit as proud and self-assured as his cousin. Richard's loftiness had got out of hand, destroying their happy relationship—that was why she had suggested they went their own individual ways for a time, until both were more mature. At least, that was the reason she had given him.

Regrets had plagued her ever since. No one else had been able to fill the gap he had left, and her heart still ached for the love they had once shared.

Back in theatre, freshly gowned and scrubbed, she took her place at the operating-table and refused to allow herself to dwell any more on the unhappiness of the past three years. Concentrating on the exacting task of assisting a surgeon, she managed well until retractors were needed to hold the skin and underlying superficial tissues back, away from the operating field. Meticulously careful to hold the retractors precisely as she had been taught, she was surprised by John's sudden outburst.

'Not that way, keep the handles up!' he barked. 'Never let them rest down so far—not when I'm operating, anyway!'

Rebecca and Anne exchanged meaningful glances. John Barrie was going to prove difficult to please, they signalled to each other. Nevertheless, Rebecca complied with his wishes. Finally, when the operation was nearing completion, she prepared to assist with scissors while he stitched the wound. She was surprised how often he seemed to glance her way. From all she could see of his face, between the mask and surgeon's cap, he was frowning. 'Your hair shows; it should all be hidden,' he grumbled suddenly.

'Male surgeons don't hide all theirs.' She looked pointedly at the brown hair escaping from under his cap to curl around the nape of his neck.

'They would if it were so distractingly red,' he returned. 'And Dr Shaw, go easy with those scissors—they're pointing in my direction. The last thing I want is to get cut and infected.'

Rebecca sighed. 'I'll be careful, Mr Barrie.'

'And cut with just the point of the scissors.'

'I'm a third year senior house officer, Mr Barrie,

well experienced with sutures—' she began in
protest.

'Well, stand back, give me enough room to
work. Try holding the thread further away from
me.'

He's impossible—quite, quite impossible,
thought Rebecca, moving away, nevertheless. As
she half feared, she now had to lean forward to
reach the stitches, and, having been on her feet
for so long already, found difficulty in
maintaining a balance. Inadvertently, her cap
came into contact with John's hand. His
immediate wrath seared through the theatre as he
called to the scrub nurse for a fresh pair of gloves.

Genuinely penitent, being well aware of the
importance of keeping surgical gloves completely
sterile, Rebecca waited with downcast eyes,
longing for her job as John's assistant to come to
an end. Once the new gloves were adjusted, all
she would have to do was hold out the suture
scissors, cut the thread when he had finished the
sewing, and that would be that. She would be
able to escape.

But, to her everlasting chagrin, her hand began
to tremble with nervousness again, resulting in
her cutting through one of his stitches, right
beside the knot he had tied, too!

Once more his anger flared—yet, to her
surprise, after taking another suture from the
scrub-nurse he suddenly handed it to her.

'*You* do the stitching this time,' he decreed,
and, after watching her at work, he turned and

strode from the theatre.

'My, my!' Sister Anne blew out her cheeks and wiped a hand across her forehead after the operation had been completed and the patient removed to the recovery-room. 'Talk about a man having a chip on his shoulder,' she reflected. 'Our new registrar has something eating away at him all right. I've never known such a disturbing atmosphere in the theatre! You and he don't seem to hit it off at all well, Dr Shaw. Why is that? D'you know? Have you met before?'

Rebecca shook her head. 'No, not that I can remember. You don't think it's simply that he dislikes red hair?'

'Yours is a glorious colour. It can't be that.' Anne dismissed the possibility, and went with Rebecca to help her change out of theatre gear.

'I'll tell you something I wouldn't want let out on the hospital grapevine,' Rebecca began, after few minutes' hesitation. 'I know I can trust you, Anne, and I need to confide in someone. The thing is, I'm engaged to Mr Barrie's cousin, Richard. In fact, we've been engaged for ages.'

'What happened? Why haven't you married?'

'Well, it was like this. Richard and I fell in love when training together in medical school. We were very happy, and had great fun with the other students. Then Richard seemed to change, and not in a way I liked. Anyway, discovering his increasing chauvinistic tendencies made me realise what my future would be like with him. My career would always have to take second place to his, which I would find intolerable, the practice of medicine being just as important to me as it was to him . . . So I told him that, and said I thought we'd better go our own ways until we had ourselves and our futures sorted out. We were to remain engaged meanwhile.'

Her carefully controlled voice revealed nothing of the deep hurt she had experienced when Richard had accepted her decision without attempting to make any sort of protest. Shrugging his shoulders, he had simply walked out of her life, never to contact her again. Her pride had prevented her from seeking him out, so she had settled for believing he would get in touch with her when he felt the time was right for marriage.

'Perhaps Mr Barrie and his cousin were very close,' suggested Anne. 'And Mr Barrie took umbrage when you rejected Richard . . . Well, *he* probably saw it as a rejection. D'you think that could be why he seems so set against you?'

'If he and Richard were close, why didn't I ever get to meet him? No,' Rebecca's anxious face broke into a grin, 'I'm sure it's my hair that makes him mad . . . you know, like showing a red flag to a bull.'

'I've heard that bulls are colour-blind.' Anne smiled back. 'But if your hair *is* the offending factor, why don't you dye it green or purple, and see what effect that has?'

'Not on your life!' Rebecca chuckled. 'But thanks for cheering me up.' And, having changed into her dress and white coat, she walked off to the surgeons' rest-room.

'Don't you forget that Mr Barrie must have thought you competent, or he would never have left you to finish closing the wound of that last op,' Anne called after her.

'True,' Rebecca replied over her shoulder, before disappearing into the room. Anne was adept at saying the right thing, she thought, glad to have had her confidence boosted by the tacit reminder that no responsible surgeon would risk leaving his patient to anyone he might fear would not be capable of doing a good job.

The rest-room was empty. Sitting on one chair, she turned another towards her and put her feet up, closing her eyes and relaxing, allowing herself a five-minute break. She would soon have to go up to the ward to see some of the new patients, then return to scrub up again, and begin work on the list of minor operations she would be doing without supervision.

The door opened to admit John Barrie. 'I thought I would find you here,' he said, walking over and looking down at her. 'You did a good job on that ectopic pregnancy. I've just seen the patient and she looks healthy enough. Congratulations.'

Rebecca looked up at him, her green eyes questioning his sincerity, then, reassured, she murmured, 'Thank you.'

He remained standing over her. 'You really have the most amazing hair.' He rested a hand on it for a brief moment. 'Quite the most vibrant shade I've ever seen. Gave me quite a shock when I came into theatre and saw some rebel strands. Your cap was all askew.'

'It was all that bending I had to do. It's a wonder my cap stayed on at all.' She looked up at him, and his deep-set blue eyes held her glance.

'Are you analysing me?' he asked finally, breaking the spell.

Feeling awkward again, she got to her feet, knocking over one of the chairs in her hurry. 'I'm just going up to the ward,' she said hastily. 'There's a patient I particularly want to see before I start on my minor ops, which today are——'

'Simple lumpectomies, removal of warts, the sorting out of sebaceous cysts . . . I know,' he interrupted. 'The list can seem never-ending. Ingrowing toenails were my special chore when I was an SHO; I used to feel that *everyone* had some and wanted to have them removed!'

'My feelings precisely.' Rebecca began to relax once more. 'However, I suppose that anything is worth doing if it relieves people's pain and anxieties. Well, I must dash——'

About to leave, she reached out to pick up a discarded theatre-cap she saw lying on another chair. 'It must be the one I left here earlier,' she was saying, when suddenly John's hand covered hers, taking hold of the cap, with her hand still in his.

'I'm keeping this cap.' He pocketed it with his

free hand, his expression serious, his blue eyes holding a puzzling challenge.

Looking at him from under her long golden eyelashes, Rebecca blushed. Then, withdrawing her hand from his warm, strong fingers, she hurried away, leaving him to pick up the chair she had knocked over.

CHAPTER TWO

ALTHOUGH now very short of time, Rebecca ran
up the stairs to Ward Eight, to see the ninety-
three-year-old patient whom Mr Hill, the
consultant surgeon, had particularly wanted her
to see.

'She's desperate to go home,' Mr Hill had said,
'but she really isn't fit to cope on her own. She
refuses all help from the Social Services, Meals-
on-Wheels and what have you. Likes to do her
own cooking, she says, and her own housework.
A remarkable little lady. Try to persuade her to
stay at least a few more days, until the results of
the tests we've carried out come through, and to
have the necessary X-rays. We want to keep her
under observation. She's a little confused.'

Rebecca was soon at her bedside, holding her
hand and talking to her.

'Get them to discharge me,' begged Mrs
Williams. 'I'm ready to go home now.'

'Not quite,' said Rebecca with a smile. 'We
haven't seen the results of your tests yet. You had
quite a bad fall, you know. We can't risk you
having another dizzy turn on the road.'

'Tests?' The wrinkled but lively face expressed
disdain. 'I know you all mean well, dear, but

19

what do tests do for you? They don't cure anything!'

'They're not meant to.' Rebecca smothered a chuckle at the idea. 'They do help to show what's wrong, though, so that the right treatment can be given.'

Mrs Williams struggled to sit up. 'They want to X-ray me,' she complained. 'I'm not going to let them. I don't see why I should let anyone see what's inside me . . . it's private. I haven't had a look myself. I reckon that if the good Lord had wanted people to see our insides, He'd have put us in glass cases, not skins.'

Attempting to keep a straight face, Rebecca glanced at her watch and, gently pressing the care-worn hand, stood up. 'I can't wait now, but *please* stay until I come back. We'll have a cup of tea together.'

'No sugar and just a little milk,' said Mrs Williams. 'Are you a nurse or a doctor? You girls all look alike to me.'

'I'm a doctor. See you later!' With a cheery wave, Rebecca hurried back to the stairs, avoiding the busy lifts because they were conveying patients, some in their beds, down to the X-ray department. She wondered whether Mrs Williams might agree to go to X-ray if kept covered by a blanket or sheet. She decided to put the idea to her, then dismissed everything from her mind in favour of concentrating on a ten-year-old girl who needed a skin lesion removed.

Scrubbed, she first operated on the girl, then

on a forty-year-old man with a similar problem, and afterwards removed ingrowing toenails from a boy in his teens, and a sebaceous cyst from a young mother.

Later, when faced with a perforated ulcer to deal with, she had no alternative but to phone John Barrie to inform him about the patient and the booking of the theatre, knowing the operation was one that only a senior surgeon would be allowed to do.

'Midnight?' growled John. 'Couldn't you have booked theatre for a more reasonable hour? I need my sleep, you know!'

'So do I, Mr Barrie,' Rebecca retaliated, tired and annoyed. 'I've been on call since yesterday, and in theatre most of the time. Didn't even get a lunch-break.'

'When you normally have a doze?' His voice was sarcastic, she thought. Very different from when he had spoken to her in the doctors' room. Resenting the change in him, she put the phone down.

Eventually finishing the minor ops list, she returned to Mrs Williams for the cup of tea she had promised to have with her. The old lady greeted her with a beaming smile.

'You're a nice girl,' she said, welcoming her. 'I've been hearing the nurses singing your praises. Sit here.' She patted the side of the bed. 'They weren't so pleased with *me*,' she whispered confidentially. 'I've been scolded, and all because I got out of bed to help with the drinks trolley!

Ah, here comes our tea.'

'Made especially for us!' With a smile, Rebecca took the cups from the nurse, and was about to offer Mrs Williams a biscuit from the accompanying plate when she hesitated. 'What about those X-rays . . . Can I take you down and get them over and done with? I promise you'll be kept covered from prying eyes.'

'I only want a sip of tea, no biscuit.'

'Right,' said Rebecca, deciding not to allow the old lady time to rebel against X-rays once more. 'Look, here's the porter with the wheelchair I ordered. *I'm* going to push it.'

'You'll take me down yourself? And you a doctor?' Gratified, Mrs Williams looked around, nose in the air. 'None of the other patients had doctors taking them down!'

'It isn't a doctor's job. I'm doing it as a favour,' Rebecca explained, helping the porter to settle Mrs Williams comfortably into the chair. Then, holding the handles herself, she pushed it towards the lift, silently signalling to the porter to stay back a little.

The X-rays over, a surprisingly compliant Mrs Williams was tucked back into her bed. 'I'll let you have tea with me tomorrow, dear,' she said to Rebecca. 'But just now I'd like to go to sleep. You were quite right, those X-rays did me good; I'm much more rested now.' Slowly her eyelids closed, so very quietly Rebecca withdrew, but not without helping herself to a couple of the biscuits left on the locker beside the bed—she was so hungry.

From then on she was kept very busy seeing emergency admissions, her bleep sounding several times. Finally, a phone call from a GP warned her he was sending in someone with a suspected acute appendicitis, so she had that new patient to check in too.

'I've hardly had a moment to breathe,' she complained to the night staff who were plying her with coffee to help her stay alert. 'And the ulcer patient should be ready for theatre soon. Mr Barrie's mad because I couldn't book theatre for an earlier time—but what can one do if others have booked it first?'

'Admin should have brought in a locum houseman to help out while Dr Martin's away. They're making "cutting costs" a top priority!' the staff nurse exclaimed angrily. 'They should just see you now—you're absolutely dead beat!'

'I think they advertised for one,' Rebecca murmured drowsily, 'but there weren't any applications. Cornwall is a bit out of the way, I suppose—especially for new doctors, who naturally want something more permanent than locum work. Oh, boy, I'm tired. I can hear my words slurring over each other. Anyone would think I've been drinking!'

At that moment John Barrie burst in, a tracksuit over his pyjamas. 'What's been done so far?' he wanted to know, his eyes blinking hard under the bright lights, as if not yet adjusted to being awake.

'All the essentials.' Rebecca strove to overcome her exhaustion. 'The patient's blood is being cross-matched, a nasogastric tube is emptying the stomach's contents, and the consent form's been signed. The patient is ready for theatre the moment the anaesthetist gives the go-ahead.'

'Right, get changed,' said John. 'I'll need you to assist.' Discreetly covering a yawn or two, he accompanied Rebecca towards the changing-rooms, endeavouring to discuss the patient's symptoms with her as they hurried along.

Too weary to make more than essential contributions to the conversation, she left him to do most of the talking. All she was hoping was that he would spare her any scathing remarks or criticisms. Her reactions, she felt, would be unpredictable to say the least.

'Been on duty long?' he asked, surprising her.

'Forty hours, and a suspected acute appendicitis case awaits my attention after this perforated ulcer case.'

'Case, case,' he echoed testily. 'Case is too impersonal. You're dealing with people, not *cases*!'

Rebecca sighed. Here we go, she mused, everything I do or say is suspect and will be judged accordingly. Hasn't he any sympathy? He knows how long I've been on duty, has had more than sufficient proof that I'm a conscientious doctor, a keen surgeon, yet still I'll be judged wrong from now on. If only there were enough theatre nurses to open another theatre, she thought wistfully, and someone else could be found to assist Dr Difficult, then I could get on with the appendicectomy, and perhaps get to bed for an hour or two. What bliss that would be!

'Dr Difficult.' The title suited him absolutely. She stole a glance at his face before he adjusted the mask. He really was incredibly like her fiancé. Just as impossibly arrogant and demanding. Yet there was a disturbingly attractive something about him to which she found herself responding, in spite of a determination not to. It was most annoying.

Carefully she pushed every strand of her fiercely auburn hair well under her surgeon's cap. At least he would not be given the chance to grumble about that, she decided.

They stood together to study the patient's X-rays. Too close together, Rebecca thought, when John rested his hand on her shoulder, yet she was unable to move away. It was almost as if he had laid a proprietorial hand on her heart. She had to force herself to concentrate on the films, even while chastising herself for being so easily distracted.

John removed his hand. 'Let's get scrubbed,' he said curtly, and Rebecca was instantly on her mettle again, dismissing her romantic feelings as mere nostalgic hankerings brought about by his uncanny resemblance to Richard.

She walked over to the operating-table, ready to assist. The scrub nurse was waiting, her runner beside her to fetch anything she might need. The atmosphere in the theatre was one of quiet confidence, edged with perhaps just a slight overtone of impatience, everyone there having a job to do, and wanting to get on with doing it.

The patient and the accompanying anaesthetist appeared. Rebecca smiled at Seema Patel, the beautiful young Indian doctor who was known to be quite brilliant at her work, and a great favourite, especially among the anaesthetic nurses she worked with, as she was always so pleasant and helpful. Everyone in the surgical unit was vitally interested in the fact that she was soon to have an arranged marriage, her parents having chosen a young man she had not yet met to be her bridegroom.

The operation proceeded smoothly, a duodenal ulcer perforation being found and repaired, and the ulcer cut in a longitudinal direction, then stitched up again in the other direction, so widening the outlet of the stomach.

A vagotomy followed, to reduce the amount of acid produced by the stomach, then, leaving Rebecca to put in a drain and close up the abdomen, John disappeared back into his changing-room, calling to her not to forget to write the patient up for antibiotics.

As if I'd forget that, she thought resentfully, sure that once again he was downgrading her as new to her job as SHO.

Still a little rattled inside, she went along to the rest-room again, this time intending to make herself a cup of tea.

'Got one for me?' John followed her in, much to her surprise, just as she was pouring boiling water over a teabag in a mug.

'There are plenty of teabags, make yourself a cuppa,' she replied testily.

He frowned at her. 'You look all in,' he commented. 'Can't you leave the appendicectomy till the morning?'

'I want to get it over,' she replied. 'There's a girl upstairs in the ward who's trying to swallow everything she can reach, determined to kill herself. I want to have time to sit and talk to her. She must be very unhappy about something or other.'

'Can't you get hold of a psychiatrist?'

'At this time of night?' Rebecca shook her head. 'Besides, I want to handle the problem myself; the girl seems to trust me.'

'Who could help it?' John put down his half-empty mug and moved to put his arm around her, again loosening her hair from her cap. 'Every time I see this mop of yours, I long to run my fingers through it,' he murmured. 'D'you think *I* need to see a head-shrinker?'

Rebecca laughed, she couldn't help it. 'The sooner the better, I'd say,' she commented. Then, to her surprise, he bent towards her and kissed her lightly on the forehead. 'That's a goodnight or good morning kiss,' he remarked, taking his arm away. 'Don't read anything more into it than that.'

The next second he had gone from the room,

leaving Rebecca to subside into a chair, her green eyes almost translucent with wonder. Then, pulling herself together, she went back to the theatre to get ready for the next operation on her list.

Finally, the appendicectomy successfully completed, she went up to the surgical ward.

'You'll never believe the things that girl has managed to get down her throat,' the night sister nodded towards Belinda, the patient Rebecca wanted to talk to. 'She must be desperate!'

'She's in pain,' Rebecca said, 'but won't allow us to relieve the pain, that's the trouble. We could do so much to help her, if only she'd let us. Anyway,' she sighed, 'I'll have another go at persuading her to stop trying to kill herself.'

Talking did little good, however, until— thoroughly exhausted—Rebecca took a stern line. 'The things you're swallowing are going to cause you a lot of suffering, much worse pain than you had before. Let's treat that pain first, then you can decide whether your life is worth living or not. You can't make a good decision in the state you're in, Belinda. Have some sense!'

Belinda stared up at her. 'No one cares whether I live or die,' she declared sulkily.

'*I* do. I care. It's my job to keep people alive. Suicide is a very negative thing. You've years ahead of you, Belinda, years in which you could do so many good things for others, or even for yourself. I know you've lost your boyfriend, but you're not alone in that. I've had rather the same experience. I know how it hurts. But we never know what lies ahead—there might be a much nicer boy waiting for you somewhere. Join the right sort of clubs, meet the right sort of people and look for him.'

Belinda's tension eased as her curiosity grew, and Rebecca took advantage of her aroused interest.

'So will you let us treat your pain and get rid of it for you?' she asked finally, taking the girl's hand in hers. 'We could, you know. But *please* don't swallow anything more than the food and tablets we give you.'

'Will you see to me yourself, then?'

'If I can,' said Rebecca. 'It depends on what you've swallowed, and whether a more senior doctor is required, but I'll be around. I'll send a porter up to take you to X-ray—that'll be the first step towards curing your pain.'

The girl sighed, but there was a look of resignation on her face, and it seemed to Rebecca that the fight was over. Breathing a prayer of thanks, she had a word with the night sister and checked that the other patients on the surgical ward were sleeping peacefully. Then she made her way over to the SHO residential block and her own tiny flat where, only partially undressing, she passed a cleansing tissue over her face and more or less fell into bed.

Two hours later she was bleeped again, so, slipping into her black leather-look flying-suit, she grabbed her white coat and raced back to the hospital. She left after a few minutes, having only had to instruct a nurse on the treatment to be given to a new admission.

With time to look at the sky, she enjoyed the rosy flush of dawn. Fluffy pink clouds threaded with gold were sailing against a turquoise background, adding colour to the grey rabbits scurrying off the grass as she approached. The world was hers, not a human in sight. She relished the pure fresh air and, slackening her steps, took off her white coat and slung it casually over one shoulder. Then suddenly, out of the blue, a voice cried, 'Hey there!'

She recognised it as belonging to Geoffrey Dunn, the anaesthetist. He caught up with her and looked her up and down, boldly appreciative.

'You're attractive like that,' he said. 'Slinky black shows off your figure and sets your hair on fire!'

'What are you doing out at this time of the morning?' Rebecca asked curiously, ignoring his remarks.

'Been to a party.' His voice slurred a little. 'I'd like to take *you* to a party; we'd have fun. You're a tempting beauty . . .' He caught hold of her arm. 'Give me a kiss, gorgeous . . .'

'Let go!' Rebecca's voice rose with her temper as she tried in vain to break free.

'Not till I get that kiss!' He managed to pull her nearer, his free arm encircling her slender waist.

'Get away from me!' Infuriated, she kicked out at his shins, but he dodged in time, without letting her go. At that moment a door burst open, and John came racing barefoot over the grass to wrest Geoffrey away and forcibly march him to the doctors' residences.

'Get indoors!' John shouted back over his shoulder to Rebecca, his voice angrily commanding. 'Can't you see the man's had too much to drink?' He didn't seem to realise that there was nothing she wanted more than to be safely back behind her own front door. Locking it, she leaned against it, feeling very close to tears. It was a bit much, she thought, not to be able to return from an on-call visit to the hospital without being accosted by one of one's own colleagues! And what was John Barrie thinking? Was he presuming she had been encouraging Geoffrey Dunn? Oh, surely not?

With no time to get back to bed, she had a shower, dressed for work, made herself a crumpet and grilled bacon for breakfast. Then, determined to put the aggravation of the early morning's unpleasant encounter as much to the back of her mind as possible, she walked back to the surgical ward to prepare for the ward round.

She supposed she would have to thank John Barrie for his intervention, but how embarrassing that would be. He must have heard her call out, his room being one of those with wide-open windows on the ground floor. He'd been wrapping his dressing-gown around him as he ran to her rescue, and his feet had been bare. He wouldn't like being reminded, so what should she say?

He met her at the entrance to the ward. Her colour rising, she faced him.

To her relief, he made no personal remarks, keeping to medical matters only, and soon they were doing the rounds, visiting patients in their beds. Not that he held back from throwing questions at Rebecca—awkward questions demanding detailed answers about the various illnesses and the surgical treatment required. However, in spite of the disturbed night and the lack of sleep, she managed to show up well.

Later, when she went down for a quick lunch-break in the canteen, Sister Anne and Staff Nurse Sue Fielding called her over to their table.

'Are you getting to know Cornwall at last?' Anne asked during the general chatter.

'Slowly. Transport's my big problem. I hire bikes on my weekends off, but the steep up and down roads defeat me. I do more pushing than riding!'

'They'd defeat anyone who wasn't a hundred per cent fit,' John Barrie said, taking an empty place at the table, and obviously overhearing. 'Don't you take any exercise, Dr Shaw? Judo would be a good idea.'

Even without the look he gave her, she would have known he was referring to her brush with Geoffrey Dunn. Annoyed at having it referred to, especially when he added, 'You can't be out chasing rabbits always. Or can you?' she snapped back at him.

'*You* should know as well as anyone that SHOs get very little time free from study and personal chores when not busy in the hospital, Mr Barrie. After all,' even to herself her voice sounded decidedly chilly, 'it can't be all that long since you were an SHO yourself!'

The crinkles at the side of his eyes gathered depth. Was he amused, she wondered, or about to wince?

Looking from one to the other, Anne butted in. 'You've a car, Mr Barrie, so why don't you take Dr Shaw for a run one day? Show her some of our rugged coastline. She'd get plenty of fresh air that way. A walk along the clifftop is as good as a tonic any time—blows the cobwebs away, as well as providing exercise.'

Rebecca stared into space, not wanting to look in John's direction or catch his eye. It was all too embarrassing for words, she told herself. Much as she liked Anne, she wished her far away at that moment. Yet, when both Sue and Anne rose and left the table, she could have begged them to stay, because they were leaving her alone with John, the last thing she wanted.

He, however, appeared quite unconcerned, and apparently fully preoccupied with his chicken and chips.

Silence reigned for several minutes, then suddenly he broke it. 'I've been thinking out the rota,' he said. 'You should be free on Thursday afternoon. We'll run down to the cottage hospital; many of our patients are transferred to us from there, or vice versa, I believe. Have you visited it? Quite near Land's End, they tell me.'

'No, I haven't been down that way at all.' She kept her eyes lowered.

'Then you must take the opportunity I'm offering,' he ordered. 'What time shall I pick you up?'

How late can I say? Rebecca wondered, not relishing spending a long afternoon in his company.

'Be ready at three.' He made up her mind for her.

She stood up. 'I ought to be back in theatre now.' She pushed her plate aside, then, remembering the objections the kitchen staff had made to collecting up dirty dishes, reached for it again. 'Can we discuss things later?' Her voice was almost pleading.

'No need,' John said brusquely. 'It's all settled. Three o'clock it is.' He studied her untouched food. 'You haven't eaten a thing . . . do I disturb you that much, Rebecca? Why? Do you know?'

She caught the teasing look on his face, and rushed away. Back in the theatre complex she tackled Anne. 'Oh, why did you have to say anything to Mr Barrie?' she burst out. 'Now I'm committed to spending hours with him on Thursday. It's bad enough coping with him in theatre!'

'Oh, did my strategy work?' Anne ignored the rebuke. 'I had said to Sue that the only way to stop him being so at loggerheads with you was for him to be given the chance to get to know you properly. Now he'll have that chance.'

'Which is a backhanded compliment if ever I heard one,' Rebecca replied, her ruffled feelings slightly mollified, nevertheless. 'However,' she continued, determined to make her point clear, 'I do prefer to choose my own company. I know you meant well, Anne, you're always so kind and helpful, but the very last person I want to spend off-duty hours with is Dr Difficult Barrie—even if I do owe him a certain debt of gratitude for coming to my aid when the anaesthetist, Dunn, accosted me so unpleasantly during the night.'

'He did? Really?' Anne was agog to hear more.

Rebecca recounted almost the full story.

'Well,' smiled Anne afterwards, 'you can't deny that Mr Barrie is your knight on a white charger. I thought he would be, given the opportunity.'

'No, no, don't jump to conclusions! You're quite wrong,' Rebecca corrected her hastily. 'He'd have done the same for any girl—any decent man would. It just happened that I was the one in need this time, that's all. He doesn't like me, he's proving that in a dozen ways, and why d'you think I've labelled him "Dr Difficult Barrie" in my mind, if not because I find him quite, quite impossible?'

'Shush,' warned Anne, an eye to the door. 'He's just gone into the changing-room behind you!'

Rebecca gasped, horrified. 'Oh, d'you think he overheard?'

'Every word,' said John Barrie, coming out and striding past, his expression more enigmatic than ever.

CHAPTER THREE

THURSDAY morning dawned bright and clear, although Rebecca had been half hoping for unseasonable fog and heavy rain, just so that the drive to Land's End would have to be put off. Several times during the morning she took quick peeps from windows on corridors or wards, only to be disappointed because the sky remained a gentle blue dotted with harmless little fluffy white clouds, while the sun shone persistently. She could think up no feasible excuse for staying in her flat in such lovely weather.

'Don't forget, be ready at three,' John Barrie had murmured as they both scrubbed up before the first operation of the day, and that was the only time he had made any reference at all to the proposed trip. For the rest of the morning he remained as offhand as ever. Annoyingly uncommunicative.

Even when the scrub nurse fainted, and Rebecca offered to take over from her because her own work in that particular operation was at an end, he said nothing. Neither a 'thank you', nor a 'don't'. She was left with no idea as to whether he was pleased or displeased with her offer.

However, she knew she was no longer needed

to assist, so went ahead and busied herself counting the atraumatics and the swabs on the trolley. Then, having checked all the other instruments to make sure they were where they should be, with everything accounted for, she turned back to the operating-table.

Conscious of John's scrutiny, she looked across at him, but the expression in his deep-set eyes was quite unfathomable, although it gave her an uneasy feeling. His mask hid the rest of his face. She was at a complete loss to know what he was thinking.

Geoffrey Dunn, the anaesthetist for the operation, was quiet too, but whether or not that was because John Barrie was there Rebecca had no way of telling. Certainly the two men had little, if anything, to say to one another.

It was an awkward, tense atmosphere. She was glad to get away from it, so, as soon as she could, she went into the nurses' sitting-room to see how the scrub nurse was getting on.

'I'm all right now,' the young girl insisted. 'I don't know what came over me. I've never fainted before, I just suddenly found myself going in a whirl of blackness. It wasn't the operation or anything—I'm too used to seeing gory things for anything like that to affect me now.' She felt the back of her head ruefully. 'I've a bump there as big as an egg—I must've gone down with a terrific wallop!'

'You did.' Sister Anne nodded vehemently. 'My back was turned, so I didn't see what actually happened, but from the noise I thought the operating-table had collapsed!'

'Supposing it had, and the patient had slid to the floor!'

'Well, it didn't, and the patient stayed put,' Rebecca said, breaking the sudden silence that filled the room, 'so we haven't that to worry about.' With gentle fingers she felt the bump on the nurse's head. 'If you faint like that again, you'd better let your GP have a look at you,' she said.

'I'd rather you did,' said the scrub nurse.

'I'm not your GP,' Rebecca reminded her with a smile. 'But I think you'll be all right now; you look fine to me. Maybe you're pregnant.'

'Oh, wouldn't that be wonderful!' The girl's face was radiant. 'Bob and I are longing for a family.' There were stars in her eyes as she looked back at Rebecca, who couldn't help envying such obvious happiness as she went off to the changing-room. She was ready for marriage herself, she felt, but how much longer would Richard keep her waiting?

It seemed ironical that she was to spend the afternoon with his cousin, when she would so much rather be with her fiancé. Would John be expecting to be thanked for his help with Geoffrey Dunn? Would she appear ungracious otherwise? Would it matter if he thought her ungrateful? She wanted to say no, it wouldn't, but her heart said yes, she needed to ride high in his estimation—not that she could figure out why. Perhaps, she thought, it was merely a matter of pride.

She tried hard to convince herself that that was all it was.

Finally the time came when she had no recourse but to get herself ready for the drive. Where was he to pick her up? He hadn't said. Nor had she any idea how long they would be staying in the cottage hospital, or whether they would be shown around. She supposed it was a good idea to make themselves known down there, however, so the outing might well achieve something.

She made herself a sandwich in her little kitchen, then thought about clothes. What to wear? Something casual? Certainly nothing special, she decided, eyeing the garments hanging in her built-in wardrobe. She wasn't going to have him thinking she had dressed up especially to please him.

A white blouse and a marine blue skirt would have to do. Although well-worn, they were crisp and neat. Knotting a triangular cotton scarf loosely around her neck, she brushed out her wealth of Titian hair and tossed it back over her shoulders. White tights, rose-patterned, with white high-heeled sandals, completed her outfit.

'You look wonderfully fresh,' John Barrie greeted her, when he called at her flat ten minutes before three o'clock.

She was glad she was ready, sure he would have criticised her otherwise.

'You didn't tell me where we were to meet, or whether you'd call.' There was some reproach in her voice. Rebecca was always on guard against being taken for granted. Richard had tended to do that, she remembered, and certainly his look-alike seemed to take her for granted on the ward and in theatre.

'That's why I came ten minutes early.' John shrugged unconcernedly. 'I knew you didn't know the arrangements.'

'Oh,' was all Rebecca could think of saying, although she was beginning to buckle a little inside. She walked to the car, determining to be just as awkward as he might be. After all, she was not on duty, and neither was he. Outside the hospital he had no jurisdiction over anything she did or didn't do. Her life outside working hours was her own private concern. If he wished to intrude into it, then he would have to take the consequences.

On this particular afternoon she was merely sharing some of her free time with him, that was all. The drive to Land's End had been his idea, not hers.

'I can feel you positively bristling,' he remarked, after they had driven in silence for a few miles. 'Is it something I've said? Can't you relax, sit back and enjoy the scenery?' His manner softened. 'You've had a rough time lately—too much work and responsibility, coupled with that unpleasant encounter with Geoffrey Dunn the other night.'

'I haven't thanked you for coming to my aid,' Rebecca said, taking the opportunity. 'I appreciated it. Dr Dunn *can* be very kind and helpful, and he's good at his job, I just don't know what got into him that time.'

'Too many pints, I'd say! Why on earth do you bother with him?'

'I wasn't given any alternative. I'd just come back from answering a bleep call when he saw me.'

'Oh, was that it? Well, take pains to avoid him in future. You don't seem to be having any difficulty in putting other people off—me, for instance.'

'*I* put *you* off?' Rebecca stifled sudden amusement tempered with incredulity.

'Yes, definitely,' he continued seriously, while skilfully skirting around a badly parked vehicle. 'But then, you can be quite an ice maiden, from all accounts.'

'From whose accounts, Mr Barrie?' she asked challengingly.

'Mr Barrie! There you go again,' John sighed. 'Always as formal and precise as a dictionary. Can't you unbend a little towards me? My name is John—as you know—and I don't mind you using it. But before we get on such intimate terms,' there was irony in his voice, 'I want to refer to hospital matters. Did you see your patient of the ectopic pregnancy this morning? I asked the nurses to call you to her.'

'Yes,' Rebecca became very serious. 'They did

call me, and after assisting Mr Hill in theatre I went up to the ward. Wendy, the girl in question, was extremely distressed—she was convinced she'd had an abortion. Her mother thought so too, and was equally upset. I saw them both and explained that in an ectopic pregnancy the baby is already dead because fertilisation took place outside the cavity of the uterus, leading to abnormal development. I think they understood. What they're worried about now is the reaction of Wendy's young husband when he hears what's happened. He's a soldier serving in Northern Ireland so she's also worried about him being over there. She's full of worry at the moment, poor girl.'

'And she didn't know she was pregnant?'

'No. She's refreshingly innocent in some ways, a very nice girl. She and Peter, her husband, long for a family of their own, young as they are—still only in their teens. I had already assured her that there's no reason why they shouldn't have the family they want, even now that she has one fallopian tube missing . . . but I don't think she was able to take in that reassurance at the time.'

'I'll have a word with her husband,' John said thoughtfully.

'Why . . . how . . . when will you see him?' Rebecca asked, surprised.

Although keeping his eyes on the road, John smiled a little smugly. 'Tomorrow morning,' he said. 'I phoned his commanding officer and asked for him to be given compassionate leave to come and see his distressed wife. He'll be flying over.'

'You did that?' Rebecca sounded amazed.

'I do have some feeling—even compassion is no stranger to me at times.'

'But why did you let me go on talking when obviously you knew all about what was happening concerning Wendy?'

'I prefer the sound of a human voice to the noise of a car engine,' John replied teasingly, adding, 'But seriously, Rebecca, tell me this . . . Do *you* want to have a family of your own?'

'Of course,' she said, looking down at her hands in her lap. 'I've always wanted at least four children, but they'd have to have the right father.'

He was quiet for a moment, then said, 'In your case, that means Richard?'

She made no attempt to reply.

Further on, he entered a lay-by, where he stopped the car and turned to her, slipping an arm around her shoulders. 'Now forget the hospital, forget Richard, and just concentrate on *me* for the next couple of hours, Rebecca,' he murmured, his voice suddenly husky. 'For years I've been thinking you already married to Richard. You, the girl I wanted to marry the very instant I saw you—only to find you were already booked. Can you imagine how I felt? Time doesn't heal that sort of heartache, believe me! Putting distance between us didn't help much either, although it necessarily eased the temptation to see you again. I had never had much to do with Richard, possibly because we were too alike in many ways, making us feel uncomfortable when we were together . . . but I was very fond of his late father, my uncle, and out of respect for him I curbed my appetite for you. I don't have to worry about that now, though, do I?'

Drawing her closer, he ran a gentle finger around her mouth, outlining its shape. 'Such pretty lips,' he murmured. 'Almost begging to be kissed,'

Looking up at him, Rebecca waited expectantly, her lips parting. She knew he intended to kiss her and was unable to resist, she wanted his kiss so much. Her whole being ached for it. For so long she had yearned to be loved again, and now, with feelings running so high, she was losing herself in a depth of warmth and passion such as she had never known before.

'Put your arms around my neck,' John was urging, his face very close, his breath hot on her cheek. 'Oh, Rebecca, I've waited for this precious moment for so long, so very long . . . I never thought it would ever come . . .'

The kiss started so lightly, it could well have been a butterfly resting on her lips, until it gathered meaning and carried her off into the realms of longing and needing, and loving . . .

Rebecca opened her eyes to gaze into deep-set blue eyes that were full of wanting, but it was John she saw, not Richard, and, realising where she was heading, she pushed him away.

His eyes lost their intensity and became veiled again. Releasing her, he started up the car, his hand shaking as he turned the ignition key.

'I'm sorry,' she murmured, not knowing what else to say.

'Sorry because you prefer Richard?' His voice was gruff. 'Oh, forget it! You want me to drive on, don't you? Then that's what I'm doing.'

Rebecca felt terrible. All the life had gone from his face, but what was she to do? She couldn't encourage him, not when things were so unresolved between Richard and herself. She hung her head, wanting to cry, almost as if she had just said goodbye to happiness.

Through narrow cobbled-stoned streets the car twisted and turned, slate and granite houses leaving very little room for vehicles to pass between them. Deeply upset in heart and mind, Rebecca began to feel physically sick as well.

'I think I'm car-sick,' she muttered, when finally the palm-tree-lined promenade of Penzance was reached, and John stopped by the Morab gardens to point out the beautiful sweep of Mount's Bay.

'You certainly don't look too good,' he said as he reached across to open her door. 'Step outside and take some breaths of fresh air. If the tide were on its way out we could walk across to St Michael's Mount, but the water's rising too fast.'

Not feeling capable of walking anywhere just then, Rebecca stayed put in the car.

John peered at her again. 'Anything I can do

for you?' he asked. 'You aren't going to be sick, are you? That would be embarrassing, right here in front of everyone.'

'Then don't look,' she snapped testily. 'If ever you'd been car-sick, you'd know how ghastly I feel.'

'I can imagine. You'd like to go down on the sands, dig a hole and bury yourself, I expect. Instead, what about having a cup of tea?'

Surprised at his understanding, Rebecca replied, 'Oh, yes, please, that's just what I need.' Then she sank back into the seat and closed her eyes, opening them only when the car stopped in the forecourt of a large hotel. Careful to avoid looking at her, John led her to one of the white wrought-iron tables on the balcony overlooking the bay.

'Talk to me,' she suggested, while sipping a refreshing cup of tea. 'Take my mind off the way I feel.'

So he told her about his previous stay in Cornwall. 'I did some of my training hereabouts, signed up with the Royal Naval Air Force. They sponsored me, even sent me to foreign countries from time to time. Also I worked a short spell with Air Sea Rescue, Culdrose. Which reminds me, I'd like to call in there on our way back to Falmouth, that's if we've time. They're a great crowd—it would be good to see them all again.'

To Rebecca's surprise, she felt a twinge of jealousy, thinking how nice it would be to bask in his approval instead of being merely tolerated, and sometimes not even that. Yet why should she strive to please him when all it would lead to would be more heartbreak on both sides, if what he had said to her earlier was true, and what she had felt was something more than she had felt for Richard?

Life was becoming very complicated.

'Did you go out on any rescue missions when at Culdrose?' she asked, to get him talking again, hoping he would reveal more about himself.

'You really want to know?' Satisfied by her nod, he recounted tale after tale about the great achievements of the rescue-helicopter teams, and what surprised her more than anything else was that not once did he include himself as any sort of hero. His praise was all for the rest of the men.

Obligingly, he continued talking even when back in the car. She knew it must have been quite a strain for such a normally taciturn man to keep up such a one-sided conversation, and had she felt better she would have been amused by the huge sigh of relief he gave when the little hospital came into view.

Going inside to reception, they met up with various doctors and nurses, then were shown around, Rebecca duly admiring the pretty, chintzy look of the wards with their dainty flower-patterned curtains and matching wallpaper.

After being given a quick rundown of the way the hospital was organised, and a rough idea of the rota system used, John prodded Rebecca.

'If we don't leave now, we won't have time to visit Culdrose,' he urged quietly, impelling her along.

She was to wish there had been no time to go there when, upon arrival, a glamorous blonde almost threw herself at him. Effusively, her arms entwined around his neck, she hung there—for all the world like a human pendant, Rebecca thought, irritated. John introduced her as 'Selena Courtney'—not that she seemed at all interested in meeting Rebecca. If anything, she appeared to resent her presence and tried to ignore her.

'John, darling.' She melted against his tall frame as if determined to be kissed, Rebecca watching, yet trying not to, and disturbed by yet another pang of jealousy. What was the matter with her? she asked herself . . . anyone would think *she* wanted John. A quite ridiculous notion!

Selena, her arm linked with his, was trying to lead him away into a nearby building, leaving Rebecca to remain by herself near the car, when suddenly, before anyone could make another move, the door of the building burst open and some flying-suited, life-jacketed young men raced out—to almost overbalance as they jerked to an abrupt stop.

'John!' they greeted him exuberantly. 'Just the fellow we need! There's an injured man on that trawler out there. Can you come?'

'Where's the usual doc?' John asked, breaking free from Selena.

'Can't track him down at the moment.'

'OK, I'll come.' Calling back to Rebecca that he would have to collect the necessary gear first, John tossed the keys of his car over to her. 'Look after my vehicle,' he told her, running into the building.

Frowning suspiciously, Selena approached her. 'What's the relationship between you two?' she asked.

'Relationship? There isn't one.' Rebecca was surprised by the question.

'Didn't think there could be; you're not exactly his type. Are you his driver?'

'No!' Rebecca found the suggestion highly amusing.

'What are you, then?'

'His assistant surgeon, that's all.'

'His *what*?' Frankly sceptical, Selena stared. '*You* can't be a surgeon!'

'That's what I often tell myself,' Rebecca said complacently. 'Nevertheless, that's what I am, believe it or not. Haven't you ever seen a female surgeon before?'

'No, and I don't believe you are one,' Selena said truculently. 'You're just trying to give yourself airs and graces.'

'There's nothing graceful about surgery. Take yesterday, for instance, when John and I cleaned out an unpleasant abscess, took off a few ingrowing toenails . . . shall I go on with the list?' Rebecca got into John's car, noticing that Selena had grown rather pale. She started up the engine and, unused to it, revved it up, making Selena jump back in alarm.

'Oh, sorry,' she called out to her through the open window. 'I didn't mean to do that. I'm not used to the controls. John always likes to do the driving; he's a very macho man, isn't he? The protective sort. I notice that particularly when we're working together through the night.'

'He might work with you, but when it comes to marriage *I'm* the one he wants. I wasn't ready to be tied down before, but that's changed now!'

Ignoring the retort, and leaving Selena to glare after her, Rebecca attempted to drive out of the car park, but the complicated dashboard controls almost defeated her. Windows, electrically operated, raised and lowered themselves repeatedly, and the air-conditioning went haywire, when all she really wanted was to indicate or reverse . . . and all this to the accompaniment of a blaring stereo radio, which defied all her efforts to turn it down. She hoped and prayed that Selena was no longer within sight or hearing!

Then, to add to her discomfiture, a sea mist began to creep inland just as she managed to manoeuvre the luxury convertible out on to the road. The mist thickened with every minute. She stopped by the wayside to search the car for a map, realising she had no real idea of the direction she needed to follow. Aware that John would accompany the injured man in the helicopter carrying him to hospital, she was sure he would not want his car left at Culdrose.

But there was no map anywhere. With visibility down to almost nothing by this time, she began to worry about the helicopter, and John in particular, fretting about whether or not he was used to coping in fog and mist. Could he have forgotten the training he had presumably received? How long was it since he had swung from the rescue helicopter?

Concerned for everyone's safety, including her own, she swung the car into a side road, thinking she might be able to discern identifiable landmarks more easily that way—only to find there were not even any centre white lines to guide her. It was unnerving having to do a three-point turn in the very narrow road, especially when the visibility was so restricted—and when U-turns became necessary on a main road she almost wanted to get out and walk!

However, after a time the mist began to lift, and soon she was able to see signposts and road-signs. Finally she spotted the hospital's tall chimney and, driving towards it, made for the staff car park.

Slowly, watchfully, she crossed to the centre reservation, ready to swerve across the road as soon as it was clear of traffic. Before she had completed the turn, however, and quite without warning, a small green car came hurtling towards her from behind the lorry she had rightly judged to be a safe distance away.

She was only vaguely conscious of receiving what seemed to be nothing but a slight bump to the back of the car—then everything went uncannily quiet.

CHAPTER FOUR

THE NEXT thing Rebecca was aware of was the sound of running feet. Then she noticed there were nurses and ambulance men around. Vaguely recalling the bump, she got out of the car to examine its back bumper, but found no sign of a scratch or dent. Relieved, she returned to the driving seat and tried to start the engine again, ready to move the car into the hospital grounds. Nothing she could do, however, could get it going.

An ambulance man approached, concern on his kindly face. 'Are you all right, miss?' he asked.

'Of course.' She wondered why he asked.

'You've had an accident. That car,' he pointed to a small vehicle stuck out in the middle of the road, 'crashed into you, and spun round in front of you, smashing everything it touched! You've had a lucky escape, but your car isn't looking so good.'

'Oh, and it isn't mine, either!' Rebecca jumped out to examine the damage. 'Did anyone get hurt?'

The man shook his head. 'Like a miracle it was, the way everyone escaped.'

'Well, thank heavens for that—but, oh, look!'

Rebecca stared aghast at the headlights hanging askew, the collapsed front bumper, the unfastened bonnet and the crumpled off-side wing. 'It's my registrar's car,' she moaned. 'He'll be furious!'

'It wasn't your fault, m'dear. I know that, 'cause me and my mate saw the whole thing happen.'

'But I can't understand it—all I felt was a slight bump in the back and there's nothing wrong there.' Rebecca sounded dazed. 'I can't remember anything else . . .'

'Retrograde amnesia, that's what it's called.' Gingerly, the kindly man helped her along, holding her arm firmly as if scared she might collapse. 'Post-accident amnesia, I'd say, 'cause so often, for some merciful reason, all memory of smash-ups in cases like yours seems to be completely wiped from the mind so it can't cause bad dreams or such-like. Often happens. Ah, here come the police. They'll want your name, address, driving licence particulars and a statement. You'd better come and sit in the ambulance.'

Following him, although still in a bit of a daze, Rebecca walked to the ambulance. 'This is just a bad dream, isn't it?' she asked hopefully when she got there.

'No, m'dear.' The ambulance man shook his head gravely. 'This is reality.'

The police asked their questions, but Rebecca was unable to answer fully, still having no recollection at all of the events immediately before, during or after the crash. What was bothering her more than anything else was what John Barrie would say when he saw the state his car was in.

She watched with some inner distress while a pick-up truck carted it away to a repair garage. It hadn't been possible to delay its removal from the road because of the hazard it provided out there.

'No one's been injured, that's the important thing,' a woman police officer remarked, accompanying Rebecca back to her flat to make her a cup of tea. 'You're very white, m'dear,' she said with concern. 'Suffering from shock, no doubt. I think you ought to see a doctor.'

'I *am* a doctor,' Rebecca put in quickly, scared one of her colleagues might be sent for—even John Barrie himself, perhaps, if he had arrived back already.

'You are? Then you ought to know the treatment you need. I'll get back to the station then, after you've drunk your tea and I've read your statement through to you.'

'There's nothing much in the statement. My mind must have gone completely blank at the time of the accident.'

'Which does happen, sometimes,' the police officer agreed. 'Nevertheless, I'll read out what little you said and you can put your signature to it, then I'll leave you to yourself. Will you be all right? Or would you prefer to have someone with you?'

'No, thanks, I'll be fine.' Rebecca needed time to work out how to break the news to John about his car being damaged.

Anne arrived after the policewoman left. 'I've just heard about the accident, came to see if you're all right.' She eyed Rebecca with some concern. 'Would you like me to make you a cup of tea?'

'The policewoman just did.' Rebecca passed a hand across her damp forehead. 'It beats me how the accident could have happened without me knowing about it.'

'Be glad,' said Anne. 'You've been saved a lot of trauma. But tell me, how come you were alone in Mr Barrie's car?'

Hesitantly, Rebecca recounted the whole story.

'He'd no right to expect you to drive an unfamiliar vehicle along strange roads!' Anne burst out indignantly. 'It's a miracle you found your way here, and another miracle that no one was hurt in the accident.'

'The mist was awful.' Rebecca's mouth pulled down at the corners. 'Supposing that helicopter crashes!'

'No, don't meet anguish half-way,' Anne reprimanded her. 'It's Mr Barrie you're worried about, isn't it?'

'The rest of the crew too, and the trawler man.'

'But especially Mr Barrie, I know,' Anne declared in her forthright way. 'Well, don't concern yourself about him, he's well able to take care of himself. But who's that Selena you mentioned? His girlfriend?'

'According to her.' Rebecca sighed wearily. 'I think I'll get to bed, Anne. Thanks for dropping in and making me think straight. I'll be all right now.'

'Have a little cry,' suggested Anne in her motherly way. 'It always helps. But remember, you've a lot to be thankful for in that it was only the car that suffered.'

'Yes, but whose car? That's the trouble,' Rebecca said wryly.

'Well, don't brood on it . . . try to get some sleep.' Anne smiled down at her while rising to go to the door. 'Things always look better in the light of day, you know that.'

'Thanks again,' said Rebecca, trying to smile, and making a move to give Anne the impression that she really was going to get ready for bed; but no sooner had Anne left than another knock came on the front door. Opening it, she found herself facing a very angry registrar.

'Where's my car?' John demanded to know. 'I've searched the car park, but it certainly isn't there!'

Rebecca bit back the tears which had just been about to fall. 'The police had it taken to a garage for repairs,' she gulped.

'Repairs? What repairs? You crashed it? I might've known—fool that I was to let a slip of a girl drive it. I had misgivings the moment I saw you with the keys in your hand!'

Rebecca swung round to face him again, tears

quelled and forgotten. '*You* had misgivings? How'd you think I felt? There I was, somewhere I'd never been before, landed with a car I'd never driven, no map, sea mist pouring all over me, blotting out any landmarks and blurring road-signs . . . yet in spite of all that I managed to get the car back here without so much as a scratch on it!'

'Then why has it gone in for repairs?' His voice stormed over hers.

'Because, because . . .' It was difficult to tell him when every time she thought about the accident she wanted to cry.

'Because, like the rest of your sex, you couldn't park it without crashing into something?'

'I object to that chauvinistic remark, and anyway, it was nothing like that. I didn't crash the car.' Rebecca collapsed on to a chair by the table, her chin cupped in her hands. 'It was an accident.' Her voice was full of misery. 'Another car ran into me.'

'You were involved in an accident?' John's anger faded instantly. 'Are you all right? Were you hurt? Rebecca, look at me, tell me you weren't hurt. Oh, my dear.' He drew her hands away from her face, and held them caringly in his own. 'What a callous brute you must think me . . . It never occurred to me that you might have had an accident. Of course you couldn't have known the way back; what was I thinking of? And to get the car here at all was quite an achievement, especially through the hazardous fog. To have had a car crash into you after all that must have been just about the last straw!'

The unexpected sympathy proved too much for Rebecca. She was in tears before she could stem them again, and the next moment found herself in John's strong arms, her head cradled against his chest, a gentle hand smoothing down her hair. He had drawn her up from her chair to stand against him, and, producing a handkerchief, he tenderly wiped her face.

Gradually her sobs quietened down, but still he held her. Then, as if desire for her was growing too strong for him to control, he buried his face in her hair.

Making no effort to break away, Rebecca closed her eyes, nestling against him, content to be held.

'I've longed to have you in my arms ever since I knew you were still free,' John murmured after a silent moment or two. 'Because Richard and I were never very close, no one thought to let me know that the marriage hadn't gone ahead. It wasn't until I finally returned to England that I found out. Can't we make up for lost time, Rebecca? Or must Richard always come between us?'

'Richard?' She echoed his name dreamily and, leaning back a little, she peered up into John's face, her vision still blurred by the recent tears. 'Richard!' She reached up and put her arms about John's neck. 'Oh, Richard, you're loving me again, and I love you. Oh, how I love you!' She raised her face expectantly, waiting to be kissed.

John froze for a stunned second, then carefully loosened himself from her hold. 'You need a sleep,' he said in a flat voice. 'It'll help clear your mind. Don't attempt to come on duty in the morning, I'll cover for you. As for the where-abouts of the car, I'll phone the police—they'll tell me. No problem there, either. Goodnight, now. Have me bleeped if there is anything you want.'

'Sorry about the car,' Rebecca muttered, hanging her head a little.

'So am I. However, it's not the end of the world.' His face softened by the semblance of a smile, if a wry one, John walked to the door, opened it and went out.

Rebecca stared after him, remembering mistaking him for Richard. A wave of embarrass-ment passed over her from head to foot. She had once again lifted her face to his as if inviting a kiss . . . what must he have thought of her? And tomorrow she would have to face him again. Even work with him!

Throwing herself across her bed, she shed a few more tears into her pillow, then fell into a troubled sleep, to be awakened half an hour or so later by a loud banging on her front door.

It was Anne. 'I won't apologise for disturbing you,' she began. 'I was talking to hubby Ted about you, and we agreed that it would do you more good to come out with us for a cheering-up drink than for you to stay here moping by yourself.'

'I was asleep.' Rebecca tried to smooth her rumpled clothes.

'Fully dressed? I know what sort of sleep that was, then. Come on, Dr Shaw, change and come along to the Grand Hotel. It's lively there.'

'What's the time?' Rebecca looked at her watch. 'Oh, it's quite early really.'

'Exactly,' said Anne. 'And now you've had a doze you'll be awake for hours, going over and over everything that happened today, which won't do you any good at all. What are you going to wear? Hurry, 'cause Ted's waiting in the car.'

'My black flying-suit?'

'Great,' agreed Anne. 'You'll turn heads in that.'

'I don't want to turn heads, as you put it,' Rebecca said. 'It's just that the Grand Hotel atmosphere and my flying-suit seem to go together somehow. And it will be quick to change into.'

'I'll give you ten minutes—meanwhile I'll wait in the car.'

After looking in the mirror and noting the effects of all the crying and worrying, Rebecca fairly plastered her face with make-up, using much more than ever before. She played about with her hair too, trying a more sophisticated style.

'See, Ted, a new look Dr Shaw,' Anne commented when she joined the couple in their car.

'Rebecca, not Dr Shaw—we're friends, aren't

we?' Rebecca suggested a little shyly, seating herself in the back.

The hotel was frequented by many of the hospital staff. She was rather dismayed to find Geoffrey Dunn there. He made a beeline for her as soon as she entered the foyer.

'Good girl,' he said. 'Plucky enough to show you haven't lost your spirit, in spite of the accident everyone's talking about. Come and have a drink. I can do with your company.'

'I'm with Sister Campbell and her husband.' Rebecca moved towards them, hoping he would take the hint and go away.

'Then it's drinks all round.' Geoffrey ordered champagne. 'We must celebrate the fact that you didn't get hurt,' he declared. 'Look, here's an empty table.'

Anne and Ted seemed pleased to be included in the mini-celebration, so Rebecca had no recourse but to sit beside Geoffrey, sipping the champagne he had paid for. Suddenly the amplifiers came to life, a small group complete with electric guitars, organ and drums, blaringly sending the latest pop tunes into every far corner of the bar. A square of highly polished flooring was cleared, and a disco began.

'Excuse us,' said Anne, as Ted drew her to her feet, 'but this is our scene. We love disco dancing!'

'Me, too,' said Geoffrey, pulling Rebecca up from her chair. 'Come on, show me what you can do.'

Never having felt less like dancing, Rebecca did her best to put Geoffrey off, but he was insistent. It was obvious that he had already had a glass or two of wine, and the addition of champagne had had anything but a sobering effect. Although she protested she was too tired to dance, he managed to keep hold of her with his free hand, even when holding a drink in the other.

Rebecca grew desperate to escape from him. Her opportunity came when she saw Anne going along to the powder-room. Making an excuse to follow her there, knowing Geoffrey could hardly refuse to let her powder her nose, she appealed to Anne for help.

'Don't you want to stay?' Anne looked surprised. 'It's so much livelier here for you, and Mr Dunn is a good dancer, I'll say that for him. We're hanging on for another hour or so; Ted's really got going!'

'I must leave now,' Rebecca insisted. 'Please, Anne. I could slip out from here to the side door without Mr Dunn noticing, but I'll need a lift back to the hospital, I'm afraid.'

'Which won't please Ted much, he'll have to do the driving—I can't, and he'll hate missing any of the disco.'

'I'm sorry.' Rebecca seemed so abject that Anne took pity on her.

'All right, you slip out and I'll talk Ted round. We'll meet you by the car,' she promised. 'Ted's a good sort, really, especially when I'm extra sweet to him, so I'll go and sugar him up!'

All three were about to get into the car when a voice hailed them. 'Leaving already?' called John Barrie, walking across the car park towards them. 'Ah, Dr Shaw . . . I thought you were having an early night.'

'We persuaded her to come out with us—thought it would cheer her up,' Anne put in.

'Then some bloke who'd had too much to drink wouldn't leave her alone, so we're running her back to the hospital,' Ted added. 'But Anne and I are coming straight back afterwards.'

'No need for you to leave,' John said. 'I'll drive Dr Shaw back.'

Ted Campbell hesitated, looking at his wife as if wondering whether she would approve.

'It's all right,' Anne explained quietly. 'He's the registrar she works with.'

'In that case . . . OK.' Ted was openly relieved. 'Come on, Anne, let's get back to the disco.'

'You don't mind, do you?' Anne asked Rebecca in a whisper, receiving a shake of the head in reply, although Rebecca was already wondering how John Barrie could run her back if he hadn't a car.

'The garage lent me a car,' he remarked, as if reading her thoughts. 'There it is.' he pointed to one with 'courtesy' printed in large letters all along its side. 'I hope you won't mind riding in it, though I can't say I'm too keen! That word emblazoned there makes it a humiliating experience.'

Something else I've made him suffer, Rebecca

thought, as she bit her lip, abashed.

'Who was bothering you in the hotel?' he asked as they drove off. 'Someone I know? Geoffrey Dunn, for instance?' He threw her an astute glance. Her colour had already risen guiltily. She had no need to answer.

'I don't understand you,' he said a moment or two later. 'I would have thought you'd want to steer clear of him after what happened recently.'

'I didn't know he'd be in the Grand, or I wouldn't have gone along there with Sister Anne and her husband.'

'Really?' He sounded disbelieving. 'You know, for an intelligent girl you seem to have a great propensity for getting yourself into tricky situations. D'you get some sort of thrill out of it?'

Rebecca was too miserable to answer. John had looked quite different in the half-light cast by the coloured lanterns strung around the car park, his likeness to his cousin Richard not at all as marked as she had thought that afternoon. What was the matter with her, mistaking one for the other? Richard's face had probably changed, anyhow. Perhaps she wouldn't recognise him any more. Would he recognise *her*?

'Were you and Richard always thought to look alike?' she asked, almost as if speaking her thoughts aloud, eager to help John realise that she had had some excuse for thinking he was his cousin, especially in her befuddled state after the accident.

'Yes,' he said, not looking at her, but concentrating on the road ahead. 'Same build—athletic, Richard called it—same colouring, brown hair, blue eyes, but it was only to be expected, I suppose, because of our fathers being identical twins. I don't know the genetics in cases like ours—suffice it to say that our resemblance to each other was something we both regretted!'

'You didn't get on with one another?'

John turned the car into the hospital grounds. Drawing up to Rebecca's residence, he shut off the engine and turned to face her. 'You didn't even notice me at your engagement party, did you?' he asked a little ruefully, adding, in what seemed to Rebecca an unexpectedly winsome way, 'And yet you kissed me!'

'Oh, I didn't!' Her eyes opened wide. 'I wouldn't have, I'm much too much of a one-man girl. I never wanted to kiss anyone but Richard!'

'When everyone was a little over-merry, party games were introduced, remember?' persisted John. 'Kid's stuff, in particular. I was sent to stand in the darkened hall during Postman's Knock, and when you came out with the pretend letter, you mistook me for Richard and threw your arms around my neck . . . very much as you did today.'

This is awful, thought Rebecca, cringing a little, although curiosity made her ask, 'What did *you* do?'

'Shall I demonstrate?' he asked, a gleam in his eye.

'No!' She moved back away from him. 'Just tell

me,' she begged breathlessly.

'Scared, are you?'

'Of course not.' She braced herself. 'Please go on.'

'Well, being his look-alike, and not wanting to embarrass you, naturally I played his part to the best of my ability!' There was enough light where they were for Rebecca to see the way he was looking at her. She blushed.

'Your kiss was quite a revelation,' he said softly.

She lowered her head in an effort to hide her face from him. 'I . . . I never knew it was you I kissed,' she said self-consciously.

'And I never forgot.'

They sat in a silence which neither of them seemed willing to break, until finally Rebecca moved to get out of the car.

'Goodnight,' John said, his voice a little strained. 'Try to get some sleep.'

'Are you going back to the hotel?'

'No. I only went there to bring you back. When I left the orthopaedic ward after handing the trawler man over, I met our theatre staff nurse. She told me that Sister Campbell intended persuading you to accompany her husband and herself to the Grand. I didn't need to be told who else would be there!'

Rebecca changed the subject immediately. 'How's the trawler man?' she asked, standing by the still-open door of the car.

'Not too bad, but some broken bones will keep

him off the trawler for a time. Anyway, you get indoors. Goodnight again.' John pulled the door to, waited until Rebecca had gone into her flat, then drove round to his own residential block.

Now, with more than the accident to think about, Rebecca made herself a hot drink and sandwich and took them into the bedroom, only to sit on her bed for a time before preparing to get into it. Even then she lay awake, quite unable to get John out of her mind. To think that, unknowingly, she had actually kissed him, and all that time ago too—three years.

And what did he mean by saying that her kiss had been a revelation?

Would she ever find out?

CHAPTER FIVE

AWAKENING at her usual time in the morning, Rebecca decided to go on duty, and not take the morning off as John had suggested before she had disgraced herself in his eyes by going to the Grand Hotel instead of having the early night he had advocated.

'Just as well you came in,' Anne greeted her when they met in the corridor. 'There's trouble on the ward. That girl, Belinda somebody, who was swallowing everything she could get hold of, is back again.'

'She discharged herself against all medical advice, mine included.'

'Well, she's in a bad state now. Came in by ambulance, and was shot straight up to the surgical ward via X-ray. Mr Barrie is with her.'

Rebecca joined him as quickly as she could.

'Why wasn't this patient seen by a psychiatrist?' he demanded angrily, showing no appreciation of the fact that she had come in to work in spite of his offer to cover for her. 'Arrange theatre urgently for laparotomy,' he barked, again reading through Belinda's medical notes.

'Look at her!' he snapped when Rebecca returned from the internal phone. 'You can see for yourself that the poor girl has a rigid abdomen.'

'She's certainly lying boardlike, although vomiting.' Rebecca bent to examine her. 'Absent bowel sounds,' she reported. 'Also low blood pressure, and pyrexial.' She turned to her houseman, Tim Martin, who had just that morning returned from holiday.

'Put up two drips of plasma substitute, Tim,' she instructed briskly. 'Take blood for cross-matching and testing.'

John hurried away to phone Mr Hill for advice, because the X-ray, just that minute delivered, showed the small bowel to be perforated by what seemed to be a crochet hook. He returned to find that Rebecca had already organised the putting of a nasogastric tube down to Belinda's stomach; a urine catheter had also been put in place.

Mr Hill came in, and soon he and John were busy operating on the girl, taking out all the various articles, such as the jewellery she had swallowed, and anything else they found which could cause trouble if left. Then they set about repairing the bowel perforation.

'Make *sure* a psychiatrist sees her when she comes round,' John had warned Rebecca before he left to join Mr Hill. 'In the meantime, take over the clinic and see as many patients as you can. There's quite a list. The two of us should have been doing it, but . . .' He shrugged. 'Maybe if you hadn't neglected to call a psychiatrist we wouldn't have needed to spend time doing an emergency laparotomy.'

Rebecca had never worked harder in clinic. Even the cups of tea the nurses brought in from time to time were left to grow cold, untouched and neglected by her. Conscious that she had been at fault in not referring Belinda to a psychiatrist, she was anxious to make up for her lapse . . . somehow it had become very important to get into John's good books.

When the clinic finished for the day she went up to the ward to see Mrs Williams, who was reported to be growing more and more restless and quite insistent in her pleas to be allowed back to her own home.

'Do what you can for me, dear,' she pleaded to Rebecca. 'You helped me so much before with those X-rays and things. I'm sure I'm all right to go home now.'

Reassuring her, without committing herself to any promises, Rebecca missed lunch in order to attend a doctors' meeting in the rest-room. To her surprise, Belinda wasn't the main subject of the discussion, but the little ninety-three-year-old was.

'The barium enema has shown she has carcinoma of the sigmoid colon,' Mr Hill informed the small group. 'If we operate, it will be an anterior resection. But do we operate? Or do we leave things as they are and let her live out her life in the peace of her own home? At her great age, she can't have many years left. Are we justified in putting her through all the trauma of a major operation? She's a very independent little lady, but would now, I think, accept the help of social workers, home-helps and the other services offered. I confess I'm very loath to cause her any unnecessary suffering, and I doubt whether, at this stage, the operation would do much for her. What does everyone else think?'

The general consensus of opinion was that Mrs Williams should be allowed home, since her heart was so set on returning to her own place.

'Will she be told what she has wrong with her?' Rebecca asked.

'Not necessarily. Not unless she asks,' Mr Hill replied, 'and somehow I don't think she wants to know. She has convinced herself that now we have treated her anaemia, which she knew about, she won't get dizzy again. Let's leave it at that.' He turned to Rebecca. 'See about getting her all the help she needs, will you? Well, that's all we need to discuss at the moment.' He rose from his chair. 'Now for the ward round . . .' He walked off with John. 'What a load of junk we took out of that girl's insides,' Rebecca heard him saying.

And she just caught John's reply, 'Enough to start up a market stall!' Then, catching hold of her young houseman's sleeve, she pulled him along the corridor with her to closely follow the two men.

'D'you like doing surgery?' Tim Martin asked as they hurried.

'Love it,' said Rebecca.

'There aren't many girls doing it, are there?'

'No, it's a man's world, and some surgeons want to keep it that way. It's going to be an uphill fight, but you wait, one day I'll gain my Fellowship of the Royal College of Surgeons, and then I'll make the dust fly. You see if I don't. Male surgeons had better watch out!'

Tim laughed with her, then they both put on sober faces and went into the ward to join Mr Hill, John Barrie, the ward sister and some medical students, in a visit to each patient in turn.

Staying on afterwards to complete some paperwork, Rebecca had a cup of tea with the nurses, then returned to her flat, where she intended to spend the evening studying for the Fellowship.

She had just made and eaten an omelette, and was busy studying a chapter on haemorrhoidectomy in one of her surgical books, when there was a knock on her front door.

Slipping her feet back into their slippers, she walked into the hall, then held back, half afraid the caller might be Geoffrey Dunn.

The next knock was more peremptory, however, so she thought she had better answer, in case whoever it was had something important to divulge.

It was John Barrie, and, without waiting to be invited in, he stepped into the little lounge and spread-eagled himself over the small two-seater settee, his long legs sprawled out before him, leaving very little room for Rebecca to get past without tripping over them.

'I'm exhausted,' he sighed. 'Any chance of a cup of coffee?'

Rebecca stepped over his legs, and went into the kitchen to fill the kettle and plug it in, all the time racking her brains to find a reason for his visit. Was it to upbraid her for recent mistakes?

'Am I supposed to make it myself, or does that apply only to the making of tea?' he called out.

'No,' she returned perkily. 'You're welcome to also make the coffee. I'm a great believer in equal opportunities for men and women. I think men should be allowed greater freedom in the kitchen, and in household chores in general.'

He actually chuckled. 'OK, you sit down, I'll make the coffee. Where do I find everything?' He followed her into the kitchen.

'It's all there.' She waved a hand around vaguely and, stepping into the lounge, took over the settee for herself, wondering how he would react to her new attitude.

Eventually he dumped two mugs of coffee on to the small table in the centre of the lounge. 'You didn't want milk or sugar, I hope,' he said. 'I couldn't find either.'

'I'm not bothered.' Rebecca picked up one of the mugs, then quickly put it down again after taking a testing sip. The coffee was cold, and much too strong. John tried his, made a face at it, and pushed the mug aside. Struggling to keep a non-committal expression, Rebecca pretended not to notice.

'I came to tell you that the insurance company is meeting the cost of the repairs to my car,' John said. 'Selena phoned the news; her father's an assessor.'

'I'm glad you won't be put to any expense.' Rebecca's remark had a note of finality about it, as if to close the subject, but that was because she wanted to exclude Selena from any further conversation.

His expression as inscrutable as ever, John studied her face. Not knowing where to look, she started to fiddle with her fingers. 'It's strange,' John said quietly, 'but when we're alone you always appear to be so on edge. Is there something about me that bothers you? I wish I knew you better, Rebecca. Where do your parents live? Have you any brothers or sisters? Do you like Indian food, Chinese take-aways, singing, gardening, painting? How do you feel about sunsets, mountains, rainbows, flowers, animals, sports, and—most important of all—marriage?'

Smiling a little, Rebecca relaxed. 'I prefer home-cooking, am captivated by the wonders of nature, and very thankful for all the music and beauty we've been given to enjoy. Lovely landscapes, cloud formations, my religion and all the other glories you mention send me into a seventh heaven of delight. I love my job too, and would of course like to combine it with a true family life, but I'd need to have the right husband first.'

'Which means Richard . . . he would be the right one?'

'I always thought so.' Rebecca looked down pensively.

'You put that in the past tense—does that mean you're not so sure now?'

She straightened as if alerted. 'Am I being interrogated?' she asked suspiciously. 'What else do you want to know? I'm a size twelve, take a four in shoes, and wash my hair once a week. I'm allergic to pollen and feathers and am an only child. An aunt brought me up after my parents died in a hotel fire when on holiday. She, too, is dead now.' She turned her head away then, the smile leaving her lips and the humour deserting her eyes.

'That's rough luck,' John commiserated, his voice sincere. 'And I'm sorry if you think I'm prying. I'm very interested, that's all.'

'It's all right.' Her face livened up again. 'Anyway, now it's *your* turn to reveal something about yourself.'

'Well, I've two sisters, both teachers, one doing voluntary service overseas. My parents are alive and well. Dad's a GP up north, and my ambition is to serve the people in the remote mountain regions . . . a sort of flying surgeon, if you like, with a mobile theatre containing all the latest equipment for life-saving operations. An airborne theatre, of course.'

'And with someone to assist?'

'Are you applying for the job?'

'Not me! You're too difficult a surgeon to please.' The words came out before Rebecca could stop them.

'Having to teach an SHO all the rudiments of major surgery is one thing, especially when lives might depend on how well that SHO has been taught,' he answered defensively, then his tone lightened, 'whereas pleasing an attractive wife is quite another thing altogether . . . Oh, but we're not talking of marriage, are we, but of work?' The look accompanying the last sentence brought colour surging into Rebecca's cheeks.

'You're blushing,' he said. 'Do I have that effect, too? But to go on with what I was saying before I digressed,' he continued nonchalantly, 'like you, I love nature, and am keen to have a family of my own. In fact I miss family life very much; I would have liked to have a brother, although I wouldn't have wanted to be without my sisters, much as they plague the life out of me!'

A close family, Rebecca noted enviously, realising how very alone she had always been. Her feelings beginning to get the better of her, she drew her book on essential surgical practices towards her, to give her something to look at, not wanting John to make some further embarrassing comment.

Taking her action as a hint that she wished to get on with her studies, he stood up. 'I'll be off now,' he said, then, looking down at the open page, 'Haemorrhoidectomy', he quoted. 'I suppose you know the rhyme meant to help surgeons when operating in that speciality? I had to quote it for my Final Fellowship.'

'What is it?' she asked. 'After all, *I* might be asked to quote it, too.' Looking up, she was sure he had gone a little pink. Certainly he seemed diffident, much to her surprise.

'I'd rather tell you in theatre,' he said. 'Anything goes in there. It's a bit different outside those four walls.'

'Please?' she begged.

He hooded his blue eyes for a moment, as if fighting shyness, revealing a side to his nature which she would never have believed existed had she not seen the evidence for herself. 'It's just . . .' John began uncomfortably. ' "If it looks like a clover, the trouble's over; if it looks like a dahlia, it must be a failure." Quote over, now I'm going!'

After hurrying to the door, he suddenly returned, bending to kiss her lightly on the forehead. 'That's another goodnight kiss,' he said. 'And this time it means more than last time.'

Rebecca closed her eyes when he had gone, wanting to picture him still there in the room with her. It was impossible to study, John had her mind in a turmoil, her heart in a quandary. If it were simply his likeness to Richard that affected her, why, she wondered, when she knew he wasn't Richard?

He had shown himself to be a sensitive person when she'd mentioned her parents and aunt, and when he'd talked about his own folk. And, she smiled, remembering, he had certainly been embarrassed about quoting that rhyme, yet one would have expected such an experienced surgeon to be hardened to the mention of such things. After all, most people suffered from piles at some time in their lives, and surgeons were always having to deal with the most intimate of health problems. But he was right, it was easier to talk freely when in theatre, hospital or clinic. In a way, it had been quite endearing of him to be diffident.

A strange man, a real enigma. Apparently prepared to marry Selena, yet making up to her, Rebecca. And he *was* making up to her, otherwise why the kisses, innocent though they were? And what about all the innuendoes? What was his objective? She only wished she knew. What was he trying to gain? A victory over his cousin? Or could it possibly be an arousing of jealousy in Selena, to make her even more eager to marry him? But, no, he wouldn't sink to such ploys, surely? He might be difficult, demanding, and even autocratic at times, but he seemed disciplined, a responsible man.

She fell asleep still thinking of him.

The next morning found her scrubbed and gowned, ready to assist before John had even arrived in the theatre complex; nevertheless, he paid her scant attention there, except for teaching and criticising.

'When elevating the tissue of the abdominal

wall by means of clips, Dr Shaw, hold them in such a way that if they spring off the tissues they won't flick up and hit me in the eye,' he insisted in his exacting way, riling Rebecca yet again by his presumption that she wouldn't know how best to hold the clips.

'You are not in any danger of that sort, Mr Barrie,' she said, as formal as he, then took extra care to do things in exactly the way he preferred, in order to avoid any more criticisms.

Nevertheless, in spite of her resolve to assist to perfection, when it came to having to cut sutures with her left hand while using right-handed suture scissors, the only ones available, all her attempts ended in failure.

'The scissors are blunt,' she excused herself. 'I can't get them to work properly.'

John's impatience seared through the theatre. 'There's nothing I hate more than avoidable delays during operations!' he declared angrily, taking the scissors from her.

She held her breath, expecting ructions, and sure enough he almost exploded with wrath when he found himself equally unable to cut with the scissors. Finally, he threw them down to the floor, demanding another pair.

The scrub nurse's runner was already fetching some.

Taking them from her, he thrust them towards Rebecca instead of using them himself. 'You finish the stitching and the cutting of sutures,' he groused. 'I've had enough!'

'He gets terribly tense when things don't go right in theatre,' Anne commented when she and Rebecca were in the changing-room afterwards. 'However, I think there was more to it than that this time. He's bothered because it said in the local paper this morning that Ward Eight's being closed!'

Rebecca stared, astounded. 'You don't mean it? No wonder he's mad, I am too! Why haven't we been told officially? Why through the press? We're short of beds already . . . Are we supposed to be cancelling patients, casually informing them that their operations can't take place? They'll all be worked up, bracing themselves to come in, making all the necessary arrangements— only to be put off at the last moment. It's cruel! I'm four beds short already; where am I going to put the emergencies? Two to a bed?'

'We're all upset about it,' Anne said gloomily, 'but what can we do?'

Rebecca charged out of the changing-room and along to the doctors' room. John, Mr Hill, another consultant and her houseman were already there, all of them storming about the untenable position they were expected to uphold. Changing her mind about joining them, Rebecca ran on to an internal phone and demanded to speak to the general manager himself. 'Tell him it's the surgical SHO, and the matter is urgent!' she said, with assumed authority.

If I wait until I calm down, she thought, I'll never have the nerve to do what I'm about to do . . .

'With reference to the closure of Ward Eight,' she burst out when the general manager came to the phone, 'why did news of it appear in the local paper before any of the medical staff had been informed?'

Taken so completely by surprise, he seemed at a loss for words.

'Well, I'm in charge of admissions for the surgical ward,' Rebecca mustered all the command she could, 'and I have four patients coming, yet no beds for them—what would you suggest I do?' To herself, she sounded like an irate sergeant-major, so she held her breath, wondering whether he would take exception to her aggressive approach. The phone seemed to go dead, then she heard voices. The general manager was speaking to someone. He picked up the phone again.

'I'm putting the bedding officer on the line, doctor—um—doctor . . .' He hesitated, not knowing Rebecca's name. 'I'm sure he will help you.'

'Thank you.' She breathed a great sigh of relief, feeling she was winning.

'Can't you cancel the patients?' asked the bedding officer.

'No way!' She was adamant. Fiercely so.

'Very well, I'll see what I can do.'

'Right,' Rebecca said. 'We shall look for prompt action!' Then, putting the phone down, she found her hands surprisingly clammy, her knees shaking. Nevertheless, she hurried back to the doctors' room, wanting to give her news before anyone left.

'I've been on to Admin,' she announced, adding a triumphant, 'Beds are to be found for our four new patients!'

'Well, that's something.' Mr Hill gave her a congratulatory pat on the shoulder. 'Now we'll write our letters of protest about the closure of the ward. A joint letter from consultants, and another from the junior doctors. Get all your colleagues to sign, Rebecca.'

Pleased to hear him calling her by her Christian name, she was only too glad to agree to do as he asked, not that she would have refused either way. She was worried about John, however; he was still looking so morose and angry, and had stayed so silent.

Suddenly, he burst out in fury. 'The whole set-up is diabolical!' he declared. 'Just think how the waiting-lists will lengthen! . . . Doctors will be blamed, the general public won't know what's going on behind the scenes . . . They'll lose confidence in us, and patients' anxieties will be doubled. The next thing to happen will be the keeping down of costs by the simple expedient of admitting no patients at all!'

'A little far-fetched, John, I think,' Mr Hill said soothingly. 'But the situation *is* serious, things will have to change.' He put a hand on Rebecca's shoulder again. 'Still, all the time we have fighters such as this young lady on our staff, there's some hope for the future.'

'Admin will probably sack me,' she maintained, 'when they find out who I am. I didn't give my name.'

'Very wise of you,' chuckled Mr Hill. 'Well, now, let's get down to the nitty-gritty of protesting. We can't just stand by and let Ward Eight be closed. Work on the letter with Rebecca, will you, John?'

'Mr Barrie's a registrar,' young Tim Martin remarked, seemingly perplexed, when he and Rebecca were alone together afterwards. 'Why is he included with the junior doctors?'

'All hospital doctors are junior doctors until they become consultants,' Rebecca replied. 'We're all apprentices until then, in a way, still being taught. That's why we have to move around so much, to enable us to get the widest possible experience in medicine, learning from our consultants, even when we're senior registrars. It's a long process.'

'I'll say!' Tim sighed. 'They never told us how many rungs of the ladder we'd have to climb before being able to settle somewhere. It was quite a shock to me to find I had to get myself a new appointment every six months. That certainly wasn't mentioned in medical school.'

'Well, you can't have been listening, then. Let's hope you'll be lucky, like me,' Rebecca smiled, 'and get on a rotation which could last two years. My contract has to be renewed every six months, just like yours, but at least I can stay here for that longer period, working in this hospital all the time, even if changing specialities every six months. I was like you at first, though, changing hospitals often.'

'I never knew I'd have to work such long hours, either,' Tim moaned. 'Double, and sometimes more than treble the hours worked by most other folk!'

'So I suppose you're going to leave and go into industry, or some other nine-to-five job?'

He grinned. 'I'm hooked,' he said, shrugging his shoulders. 'I still want to be a doctor, no matter what.'

'Same here—I wouldn't want to be anything else,' Rebecca affirmed. Then she was silent, knowing there was something else she wanted to be besides doctor and surgeon. Something she was beginning to long to be. Longing so much that it was like a persistent ache inside her.

CHAPTER SIX

THE FORM the ward closure protest should take was roundly discussed during the next week until all involved in surgery, from consultants downwards, agreed on the format to be adopted, and John and Rebecca could proceed with the task of composing the strongest possible letter voicing all the disapprovals and suggested alternatives.

When quite satisfied with their combined effort, Rebecca gave it to Mr Hill's secretary to be typed out, then took the finished product for John to vet and show to the senior doctors.

'Since you have to wait before collecting the other signatures, I have something to suggest,' he said.

She waited, wondering what it could be.

'It's about the car I've hired—quite a beauty. Come and test it tonight. I'll pick you up at eight. Just say yes, you'll be ready when I call.'

Rebecca looked up at him and found herself saying, 'Yes, I'll be ready when you call,' almost as if the words had a mind of their own.

'Good.' John seemed to take her compliance as a matter of course, going on to remind her that he wanted her to assist at the next operation which was due to start in fifteen minutes, so she had better hurry.

That man is quite, quite impossible, and quite impervious to any plans other than his own, she muttered to herself as she flew along the corridor, seeking other junior doctors to warn them that the letter would be coming around for their signatures after the consultants had approved it. Why should she be the one John wanted to show his car? she wondered. Why not Selena? Surely it should be *her* privilege, if privilege it could be called.

She was careful to return to theatre in time to get scrubbed ready to assist, and this time was not at all surprised to find John Barrie very much all surgeon again.

'Retractors!' he ordered imperiously. 'And please hold them correctly this time!'

The operation proceeded much as usual after that, except that she was allowed a far greater share in the actual surgical work involved, much to her satisfaction. She felt as if John must be gaining confidence in her ability, otherwise he would never have risked letting her do as much as she did.

Eventually, when the day's work was through, Rebecca went to her flat to get ready for the evening drive. Taking great care with her make-up, in an effort to hide the pallor of exhaustion which still tended to take over on her face, she added a delicate touch of pink blush to her cheeks, then brushed her beautiful auburn hair until it shone like deep amber, the midnight blue of her silk trouser-suit providing the perfect background to show it off.

John called for her, and, when she answered the door, stood stock still gazing at her, his eyes half-veiled, as if peering at a masterpiece and trying to get every last detail into focus.

'Let's go.' He caught hold of her arm.

'Wait a minute, I have to lock up,' she said breathlessly, very conscious of an undeniable electricity in the air between them, an appeal emanating from him, from his touch on her skin, from his manly strength, from the face that was so like Richard's. Her heart started playing tricks again, and when, in the car, he leaned across to fasten the seat-belt around her, his head coming very close to hers, it took the greatest effort on her part to back away from such close contact with him.

Adjusting his own seat-belt, he started up the engine and raced the high-powered limousine away into the night. A clear, starry night, a full moon casting its silvery brilliance over the wide landscape.

'A night for romance,' John murmured. 'Are you a romantic at heart, Rebecca, or only where Richard is concerned?'

'I favour romance,' she replied evasively. 'Most girls do.'

He drove into a lay-by, parking there and losing no time in putting an arm around her shoulders. 'I'm not made of ice, you know.' His voice was strained. 'Can't you forget my cousin for just one evening? He might never return to you, Rebecca, have you considered that possibility? One has to face facts, to take reality into account. Will you wait for him all your life, giving up all chance of achieving what you desire in other directions not connected with medicine?'

'Richard *will* come to me,' she declared stubbornly. 'He'll be a changed person, more mature and understanding . . . all the things I wanted him to be. Time will have helped develop him.'

'And the two of you will go off into the sunset together, to be happy ever after? Oh, come off it, Rebecca . . . your head is in the clouds where Richard is concerned!'

In answer she put up a hand and lifted his arm off her shoulders, pushing it down by his side, then edged as far away from him as she could.

Without another word he drove out of the lay-by, then sped towards the A30 carriageway and up across the lonely, desolate Bodmin Moor. Suddenly, he made an emergency stop.

'Why, what's wrong?' gasped Rebecca who had been lost in her thoughts.

'One of the wild moorland ponies decided to try to cross in front of us . . . Whew,' John blew out his cheeks, 'that was a near thing! Are you all right?'

'A slight touch of whiplash.' She rubbed her neck where it hurt. 'Otherwise OK. You too?'

'I'm fine, but I could do with a drink. Look, there are the lights of Jamaica Inn, shall we stop there for a bit of a break?' He drove on without waiting for her to answer, and turned in off the road under the inn-sign depicting the uncouth and grim-faced smuggler, Joss Merlin, who scowled down from under a tricorn hat, a menacing, brooding eye cast on all who passed, his other eye covered by a black patch.

As John led the way to a great wooden door in a porch, huge drops of rain began to splatter the courtyard, and the wind rose. Rebecca looked back over her shoulder as the inn-sign swung and creaked eerily. She shivered. 'Clouds are building up,' she remarked. 'Huge thunder clouds!'

'Come in and get warm,' John said, walking her into the large stone-flagged lounge. A roaring log fire blazed invitingly, its flames reflected from the many types of brassware hanging from the old oak beams roofing the spacious room.

Finding the heat rather too much for her, Rebecca wandered away into Mary's bar, John following to take a seat beside her on a high-backed wooden settle.

'What would you like to drink?' he asked. 'A pot of ale would fit in with the surroundings! Did you notice all those brandy kegs in Joss's bar?'

'Lemon and lime for me, please,' she insisted.

'I suppose I had better have something non-alcoholic, too,' he sighed.

A girl dressed in keeping with the inn's bygone days came to take the order, and recommended the home-baked Cornish pasties, so was asked to bring two of those, too.

'I've tried the original recipe,' John remarked after she had gone. 'Meat and vegetables in one half, cooked fruit in the other, just as the miners' wives prepared them for their men in the old tin-mining days. What days those must have been . . . there was no Women's Lib then—women were content to stay in the home and bring up the children.'

'Serving their lord and master meanwhile, I suppose?' Rebecca put in a little sourly. 'Who wants to go back to the bad old days? I don't.'

The order was served, and she tried the pasty—a modern version without fruit.

'They're good, aren't they?' John took another bite of his.

'Mmm,' said Rebecca, agreeing with him for once. 'But what a size! They overlap the rims of the plates. It'll take me a month of Sundays to eat all this!'

'We can't wait *that* long.' John's touch of humour seemed to ease away the awkwardness there had been between them before, and Rebecca was glad, thinking it a sign of an easier relationship building up between them. Especially glad when, just as they were leaving the inn, a vivid flash of lightning startled her to such an extent that she literally threw herself into his protective arms, much to her embarrassment.

'Oh, I'm sorry,' she said the next second, 'but I hate storms!'

'*I'm* not sorry.' John's arms tightened around her as he drew her back into the shelter of the porch. 'Let's stay here until the storm passes.'

'No, I mustn't be silly.' She pulled away from him. 'One can't give way to one's phobias . . . oh!' She jumped back to him as another flash was immediately followed by a violent crack of thunder rending the air.

So closely did John hold her this time that she could actually feel the thud of his heartbeat. Relaxing against his strong chest, finding comfort in his nearness, she stayed still.

'Rebecca,' he murmured, tipping her face up towards his, 'this is John holding you, not Richard—please realise that.'

She bent her head, resting it against him again. 'I know,' she said. 'I know.' But her voice was sad.

Releasing her slowly, John merely remarked that the storm seemed to be passing, and that it might be as well to dash out to the car before the rain became heavier.

As he fastened her seat-belt again, he muttered something to himself.

'What did you say?' Rebecca asked.

'Nothing much. I was just reminding myself how pleasant it was to hold a girl in one's arms.'

'Like when you held Selena at Culdrose?'

'I think it was more a case of her holding me, if I remember rightly.' He sounded amused. 'Mind you, she's a very attractive girl.'

Rebecca gazed out of her window as they drove along. Great tear-like raindrops obscured her view, running down the glass. Now and again she could see beyond them to the deepening pools of water accumulating along by the grass verges, all of them spurting up little fountains as the heavy rain fell into them. The outlook was so miserable that she blamed it for the tears which were welling up at the backs of her eyes. John was behaving atrociously if one really thought about it. Not content with having Selena, he was now making passes at *her* and, not only that, he was doing his best to undermine her confidence in Richard. It was a mean thing to do. Of course Richard would return to her. Their parting had only been a temporary one. The engagement remained unbroken; she still had his ring.

However, John was right in some respects. Years had passed without sight or sound of Richard. There had been no further contact between them. She had thought it best to make the break complete at the time. Now she was beginning to have her doubts. Richard could have traced her, had he wanted to. Was he waiting for her to make the first move? Could she run the risk of further hurt? Supposing she met with a rebuttal?

A tear actually escaped to run down her cheek at the very thought.

'Are you all right?' John asked, as if sensing her unhappiness.

'Fine,' she said, swallowing hard.

'You like the car?'

'It's fine.'

'And the evening . . . has that been fine too,

in spite of the mishaps?'

Again she thought she detected amusement in his voice, and wondered if he were laughing at her. If so, he was pretty callous—perhaps heartless would be a better word. There could be no real friendship with such a man.

They stopped outside her flat, but she didn't invite him in for a coffee, although she had intended to. Somehow the thought of Selena had disturbed her once again. All she wanted was to be left alone for a while, alone with memories of the happy, carefree days when she and Richard had enjoyed life together.

'I think I'll go straight to bed,' she said to John as she got out of the car. 'I'm very tired and it's rather late. But thank you for the ride and the supper. The car is really great.'

'But would be even better if it had another driver . . . someone called Richard, for instance? I know, you don't need to tell me. Well, goodnight, see you in the morning, Rebecca. Get a good sleep—don't let regrets keep you awake.'

'He knows me too well,' she told her curtains as she drew them over the windows. 'Reads me like a book. It's *very* embarrassing.' Taking a last peep through the gap left between her bedroom curtains, she noticed that stars were out once again, and the rain had completely stopped. Broken clouds hastened across the night sky, as if in a rush to meet up with the storm clouds now far away on the horizon. Here and there a moonbeam struggled to break through the scurrying clouds. She watched for a further minute or two, then drew the curtains fully and prepared for bed.

The next morning was 'business as usual' as far as John was concerned. With a brief nod to her, he continued with his ward round until he had seen every patient needing surgery, discussing their symptoms with her in a professional way, remaining absolutely impersonal. Finally, when they were walking away from the wards together, he said 'It's time you learnt to do a cholecystectomy by yourself. I'll talk you through the operation. Hopefully it'll be a straightforward gall-bladder removal.'

Thrilled about the chance she was being given, yet a little anxious in case she incurred his anger again, Rebecca, scrubbed and gowned, waited while John prepared for the operation. Then the patient was brought in from the anaesthetic-room.

Under John's guidance, Rebecca did a Kocher's incision, cutting the patient just under the right costal margin.

'Just under the ribcage.' John checked. 'That's good. Now what?'

'Diathermy,' replied Rebecca, starting to burn the blood-vessels by means of the small electric current, touching them lightly, but enough to stop any blood from oozing out.

By this time she was feeling competent, knowing exactly what to do, having watched several similar operations and assisted at quite

Temptation novels bring you all the joy and tenderness of age-old romance, experienced in contemporary love affairs...

And to introduce you to this powerful, highly charged series, we'll send you *4 Temptation books* absolutely **FREE** when you complete and return this card.

We're so confident that you'll enjoy Temptations that we'll also reserve a subscription for you, to the Mills & Boon Reader Service, which means you could enjoy...

- *FOUR BRAND NEW NOVELS* – sent direct to you every month (before they're available in the shops)
- *FREE POSTAGE & PACKING* – we pay all the extras.
- *FREE REGULAR NEWSLETTER* – packed with special offers, competitions, author news and much, much more...

FOUR
IRRESISTIBLY
CAPTIVATING
NOVELS
FREE!

★☆ **PLUS** ☆★

YOURS FREE!

This charming pair of glass oyster dishes exquisitely modelled to add a pretty touch to your home. You can store precious little things in them or keep them handy for sweets or nuts.

★☆ **PLUS** ☆★

A SURPRISE
MYSTERY
GIFT

▶▶▶▶ **CLAIM THESE GIFTS OVERLEAF** ▶▶▶▶

FREE BOOKS CERTIFICATE

Yes! Please send me my **4 Free Temptations** together with my **FREE GIFTS**. Please also reserve a special Reader Service Subscription for me. If I decide to subscribe, I shall receive 4 superb Temptations every month for just £5.40 post and packing free. If I decide not to subscribe I shall write to you within 10 days. The free books and gifts will be mine to keep in any case. **I understand that I am under no obligation whatsoever** - I can cancel or suspend my subscription at any time simply by writing to you. *I am over 18 years of age*

8A9T

NAME _____

ADDRESS _____

_____ POSTCODE _____

SIGNATURE _____

FREE GIFT

Return this card now and we'll also send you this 2 piece glass dish absolutely Free together with....

A SURPRISE MYSTERY GIFT.

We all love surprises, so as well as the FREE books and glass dishes, there's an intriguing mystery gift especially for you.

POST TODAY!

MILLS & BOON
FREEPOST
P.O. BOX 236
CROYDON
CR9 9EL

NO
STAMP
NEEDED

a few. All the same, it was different being the
surgeon herself, John merely assisting. He was
holding the wound open with retractors, a job she
usually had to do. Thinking how critical he had
been towards her, her hands shook a little
nervously.

'Watch it, control yourself,' he warned,
noticing. 'Don't let your concentration waver.
Forget all about romance.'

His words stung her into a greater
determination to do everything as it should be
done, and not only for the patient's sake, but to
prove to John Barrie that she was efficient, and
capable enough to manage on her own without
his guidance. She knew she had been given the
gift of a certain surgical skill. It was time, she
thought, that he recognised it as well.

Romance, indeed! Was that all he thought she
thought about? It seemed so from his frequent
comments. But he must know there was more to
her than that. He knew she was studying for her
full Fellowship of the Royal College of Surgeons,
so must realise that she already had her Primary
Fellowship, which also took some getting. Hard
work and deep-seated learning had paved the way
to it, plus concentration.

She would show Mr Superior John Barrie that,
apart from anything else he might choose to
think, she had the ability to become a really
skilled surgeon.

Even as these thoughts ran through her mind,
she was getting through to the patient's

abdominal cavity and, taking a quick look at the gall-bladder, she felt the stones, then checked the liver, while allowing air to go between it and the diaphragm to slightly mobilise the liver.

After checking the stomach and duodenal for any sign of ulcers, she ran an exploratory hand over the large bowel and into the pelvis, checking this time for any obvious tumour, although not expecting to find any.

'Nothing there?' John asked.

Shaking her head, Rebecca got on with the operation, dissecting and tying the cystic duct and blood vessels, John watching.

The radiographer being already on hand with an X-ray machine, Rebecca injected radiolucent dye into the ligated cystic duct, knowing it would show up on the films.

'All right,' John said a few minutes later. 'Now you have the X-ray of the biliary system, look to see if there are any stones in the common bile duct.'

'Which is just what I'm doing, and the bile duct is clear.' Without giving him a chance to issue more instructions, she proceeded to dissect the gall-bladder away from its liver bed.

'Secure haemostasis!' John barked the order, but Rebecca was already rechecking that everything had stopped bleeding, including the liver bed. When all was satisfactorily dry, she put a couple of drains into the abdomen and stitched it up, John Barrie watching still, but making no further comment.

Taking the gall-bladder, the nurses opened it up and took out the stones, washing them and putting them into a little jar for the patient to see when fully conscious again. Then they sent the gall-bladder to histology.

Relieved that everything had gone so well, Rebecca took off her green gown and surgical gloves, then wrote up the operation notes.

Looking up at all she could see of John's face between mask and cap, she thought she could detect approval in his eyes. Catching her glance, he patted her shoulder. 'Remember to put *your* name down as the surgeon,' he said. 'You did a good job. Now I suppose you're feeling proud of yourself, and in need of a cup of coffee? Come along to the surgeons' room, I want to talk to you.'

So he did find something to criticise, Rebecca thought, disappointed. Well, at least he had the decency to want to tell her in private. She followed him a little unwillingly. She could hardly tell him that he had proved a distraction just by being beside her during the operation, that she would have managed even better without him looking over her shoulder or assisting. He would only remind her that, had someone in authority not been there with her, she wouldn't have been allowed to do the operation at all. And he would be right, of course.

It was not as if it had been one of the minor ops which she could do by herself, having already been taught how to do them. Having successfully completed many, she was now faced with having to have John teach her the more major operations, which inevitably meant spending more time with him. There would be no way of avoiding him, if she wanted to learn. And she did. Besides, he was an excellent teacher, she had to admit it.

Sister Anne waylaid her along the corridor. 'Now you can add cholecystectomy to your list of successes,' she began, congratulating her. 'I think that's one of the most complicated of operations, there's so much for the surgeon to see to. You'll find your appendicectomies a mere piece of cake after that!'

'It rather depends on the state of the appendix, doesn't it?' Rebecca replied thoughtfully. 'There was that girl earlier this week who'd left having surgery almost too late. That was a horrible challenge.'

'Well, she's OK now. Which reminds me, what happened to the young woman who was swallowing everything in an attempt to commit suicide?'

'All the objects were removed in a successful operation,' Rebecca told her. 'But then what'd you think? She went home and, a short time afterwards, took an overdose. She's in a psychiatric hospital now.'

'An overdose? How terrible,' Anne sobered, her face saddening. 'Well, I suppose we can't win them all. Let's hope now she'll get the help she needs.'

'Mr Barrie's waiting for me, I'd better go,' Rebecca sighed, looking a little depressed.

'He is? I wonder what he wants. Anyway, don't take anything he says too much to heart. You're a good surgeon, and I should know—I've watched dozens of them at work—so stand up to him, Rebecca, give as good as you get!'

Her ego slightly boosted, Rebecca hurried along to face John. To her surprise, he made no mention of the operation. The closure of Ward Eight was the subject he wanted to discuss.

'One of the other registrars was unable to complete his list of ops yesterday, because, although he and the assisting houseman and the anaesthetist were all scrubbed and ready, the nursing officer refused to allow any nurses to staff the theatre, saying that as the op would go on until after five p.m. when day-nurses go off duty, they couldn't assist, he wouldn't allow it. The patient was actually prepared and waiting too! There's a bad atmosphere permeating the hospital, and I put it down to the closing of the ward. Having to search out our patients now they've been distributed all over the place is time consuming, to say the least!'

'I wonder if our letters of protest have had any effect on Admin?' Rebecca said thoughtfully. 'Perhaps more could be done in that line.'

'You're prepared to continue fighting? Good for you!' John caught hold of her hand and, at that moment, Geoffrey Dunn walked into the room.

'Am I interrupting something?' he asked, looking from one to the other.

John immediately released Rebecca's hand and, made self-conscious by Geoffrey's suggestively raised eyebrows, she stood aside.

'Apparently I was.' Geoffrey threw his lanky figure into the nearest chair. 'Come and sit on my knee, Rebecca.' His strangely lopsided smile was obviously meant to be inviting. 'That's if John can spare you?'

John glowered, so, trying to ease the situation, Rebecca merely answered with a mild, 'I don't make a habit of sitting on anyone's knee.'

'Which is a pity,' Geoffrey rejoined, 'because I'm sure our glum registrar is angling for some form of physical contact with you——'

'You're being very offensive!' John marched from the room, anger in every line of him.

'Funny fellow, always so incredibly touchy,' Geoffrey sighed.

'Always?' Rebecca helped herself to a mug of coffee from the jug left ready on the low table and waited, her curiosity aroused.

'Always,' repeated Geoffrey. 'I've known him since we trained in the same medical school. Didn't get along with him any better then than I do now. He was a stickler for keeping to the rules, whereas I considered there ought to be more to life than constricting regulations. A bit of a rebel, I suppose, but no real harm in me. I simply liked my bit of fun.' He eyed her impudently. 'You'd be great to have fun with, Rebecca, if only you'd loosen up on your inhibitions.'

'What makes him "touchy", as you put it?' she asked, ignoring his last remark.

Geoffrey gave a knowing laugh. 'So, you're the one doing the angling now, are you? Want to find out more about your precious John?' His thick lips curled unpleasantly. 'Then I'll tell you something you'd rather not hear. He's either secretly married, or about to be.'

'I don't believe it,' she declared stalwartly, her heart sinking, nevertheless.

'A fact remains a fact, whether it's believed or not,' Geoffrey declared.

'To whom, then?'

'Some blonde,' he replied nonchalantly.

'From Culdrose?'

'Ah, you know about her already? I met her last night at a dance.' Geoffrey rose from his chair. 'Well, don't let on I spilled the beans, or there'll be ructions.' Replacing his coffee-mug on the table, he hastened from the room, an air of unease about him, although Rebecca was too disturbed to notice—she was having difficulty enough taking in the implications of the news she had just been given.

John and Selena married? She slumped back in her chair. Oh, surely not? Yet how many men had been captivated by girls like Selena? Dumb blondes, they might be called, but they weren't so dumb when it came to beguiling a man of substance . . . and no one could say John wasn't a man of substance. Selena would know instinctively how to weave a web around him, a web from which he would have little chance of escape. And he probably wouldn't even notice he was being trapped. Being trapped . . . or already trapped?

Chastising herself for letting the question bother her, she went up to the wards after a snack lunch, to seek out her patients and instruct Tim about the jobs she wanted him to do for them.

'There are seven miles of corridors in this hospital,' she told him. 'I can see where all my energy will be used up. I'll be completely exhausted by the time I get to theatre. It's too bad our surgery patients have been so widely distributed all over the place.'

'I won't be needing my squash or badminton to help keep me fit,' Tim sighed. 'It'll be a case of running a marathon all day long.'

'Walking, not running,' Rebecca advised, amused. 'We wouldn't want to alarm the patients. They'd be thinking the hospital was full of cardiac arrests!'

The rest of her day was too busy for her to even have time to wonder where John had got to, or to fret about the news Geoffrey had given her, but in the evening she had a surprise visit.

'Selena's here,' John said at her door, a harassed look on his face. 'Could you put her up for the night?'

Rebecca's heart sank at what she saw as evidence substantiating what Geoffrey had said. Ushering the couple into her small lounge, she quickly tidied away her books and papers and offered to make tea or coffee, all the time fighting an inner distress.

'No drink for me.' John moved back to the front door. 'I can't wait. Selena might like one, though.' He turned to her. 'You've brought your overnight things with you?' he asked.

'Of course.' She gave him a slow, meaningful smile.

'I'm off, then.' He opened the door. 'Can't keep the patients waiting,' he added with a relieved air as he stepped out into the night, closing the door behind him.

'What patients?' Rebecca asked Selena, knowing of no emergency. But if there were, she was thinking, that would explain why he had brought Selena to her. Quite possibly the girl was nervous about sleeping on her own in a strange place, and if John had to be busy in theatre for hours, as was possible, then . . . She put the shutters down on her conjecturing, unable to reconcile herself to the thought that Selena had come prepared to spend the night in John's flat. Yet, if they were indeed husband and wife, what could be more natural? She fought against the sadness she felt at the thought of him being married, but the unhappiness remained.

'Are you married?' She blurted out the question before she could stop herself.

'To whom?' Selena looked wily, obviously on her guard.

'To John, of course.'

'Is that what you've been told? Did he tell you

himself?'

It was plain to see that Selena had no intention of giving anything away, so Rebecca let the subject drop rather than risk giving the knife another twist in her heart.

'I must have a bath.' Selena looked around. 'You do have a bathroom?'

'And water. We are quite civilised here,' Rebecca found herself replying.

'Good,' said Selena, not noticing the sarcasm.

'What about something to eat?' asked Rebecca.

'I'll have supper in bed.' Without more ado, Selena collected up her pyjamas, requested a clean towel, and disappeared to find the bathroom.

'Is this where I'm to sleep?' Coming out afterwards, she walked into Rebecca's one and only bedroom. 'Have clean sheets been put on the bed? I'm exhausted,' she said, yawning. 'I'd better have supper right now, or I'll be too tired to eat. What have you prepared?'

'Nothing yet. What d'you want? I'm tired, too, I've been on duty all day.'

'Yes, but *in* the hospital, whereas I've been outdoors walking my feet off around a golf course. An egg on toast would do me, as long as the egg doesn't make the toast soggy—I hate that.'

Keeping her temper only with difficulty, Rebecca prepared a supper-tray to take in to her demanding guest, then spent the most uncomfortable night of her life curled up on the hard cushions of the two-seater settee. The cushions parted company every time she turned, and her legs had nowhere to go, so hung over the wooden arm-rest, while she pillowed her head on the other arm-rest, giving herself a chronic crick in the neck.

She was still awake when the knock came on her window at the break of dawn. Drawing back the curtains, she found herself faced by John, his head haloed by the pearly glow of the rising sun.

'Tell Selena I'll run her back to Culdrose, but we'll have to leave within half an hour—I must get back for my ward round,' he called quietly through the half-open window. 'But take over the ward round if I'm delayed, will you?'

So, he's again showing confidence in me, Rebecca thought, and she warmed to the compliment as she went into the bathroom to awaken Selena.

'John's waiting to drive you back to Culdrose,' she told her.

Selena blinked drowsily at the bedside clock. 'At this unearthly hour?' she complained. 'The man must be crazy!'

'He's got to get back in time for a ward round.'

'Oh, tell him to take the day off!' Selena turned on her side as if to settle off to sleep again.

Rebecca rebelled. 'There's a certain discipline to medical life, you know. We can't just do as we like, we have the patients to consider. Ward rounds are essential—as essential as the operations themselves. It's vitally necessary to assess the condition of patients both before and after ops——'

'Oh, don't preach,' Selena groused. 'I'll be glad to get up and leave here, the way things are . . .'

Rebecca grilled her last piece of bacon and last tomato, and toasted her last two pieces of bread, placing everything before Selena. There was nothing left for her to have herself, shopping having been impossible because of the long hours she had been working.

'Do you always take only a cup of tea for your breakfast?' Selena asked, and, not waiting for an answer, went on to grumble about John. 'I hope he'll be in a better mood than he was yesterday. Hardly spoke a word to me when he found me up here. Seemed to want to hide me away . . . oh, that'll be him now,' she added as a peremptory knock came on the door.

Having cleared her plate, she collected her overnight bag and waited.

'John, dear!' she gushed as Rebecca opened the door to him. 'I wouldn't have got up this early for anyone else!' Her upturned face waited expectantly for his kiss.

'Oh, we're embarrassing what's-her-name,' she said, glancing triumphantly over her shoulder as Rebecca involuntarily turned her back. 'So, come on, let's get out into the car where there's more privacy.' Handing John her travel-bag and drawing him away from the flat, she called out, 'Thanks for putting me up,' then smiled up at John as if hoping he had noticed how nice she was being to Rebecca.

Putting her up . . . or putting up with her? Rebecca grimaced ruefully as she surveyed the disturbance inside her flat. Selena had certainly had a turbulent effect . . . in more ways than one!

CHAPTER SEVEN

'I GATHER that John's taken the little woman back to base.' Geoffrey Dunn settled down beside Rebecca in the doctors' room, where she was giving her few spare minutes to familiarising herself with the names of some surgical instruments she had yet to come across. 'Quite a glamour puss, isn't she?' Geoffrey added.

With a sigh of defeat, Rebecca closed her textbook of surgery. Geoffrey was unlikely to allow her to continue studying, and, in any case, her next patient would soon arrive in theatre awaiting operation.

'I don't know why a girl with your looks has to bother with all that stuff.' Geoffrey tapped the book with his long fingers. 'You'll be married and bringing up a brood of children before you can make use of a Fellowship.'

'Think so?' Rebecca replied laconically, not really interested in his opinion.

'Unless of course your heart is set on someone else's husband?'

Her colour rose, in spite of her attempts to stay cool and calm.

'But, no,' Geoffrey shook his head, 'you're too honourable for that . . . so, as I'm still free and very interested, what about giving me a chance, Rebecca? I'm not a bad bloke at heart.'

He caught her hand when she remained quiet. 'Listen, gorgeous, I'm taking you out on Saturday night. A dinner-party in a hotel, lots of my friends will be there all clamouring to meet you. It'll do you good to merge with people outside the hospital environment. I'll collect you at seven. I've already checked that you're off duty that evening, which just goes to prove how keen I am, doesn't it? Oh, and by the way, it's a best bib and tucker affair . . . so dress to kill!'

Drawing her hand away, nevertheless, Rebecca hesitated. Perhaps Geoffrey was trying to be kind? He must have guessed what a strain it had been, having Selena thrust upon her for the night. Anyway, she should give him the benefit of the doubt—that was the least she could do.

Besides, she thought, while walking to the door, indirectly he was giving her the longed-for chance to show off her long evening dress.

A dream of a dress, it had cost what to her was quite a fortune. Just seeing it hanging under its plastic cover in her wardrobe made her feel like a million dollars, so what would the feeling be like to wear it where other people could admire it, too?

She smiled back over her shoulder at Geoffrey. 'If evening dresses are to be the order of the day, I'll come,' she promised.

'Personally, I'll be wearing a suit,' he replied facetiously.

At least he has a sense of humour, she consoled herself, rushing down the corridor to the theatre. The day had been a busy one for her. John Barrie still being missing, she had taken his ward round, held a clinic, and since then had started on a succession of hernia repairs as soon as the patients had arrived and were made ready. There had been no time for lunch.

'Gone are the idyllic days when surgeons could order it to be sent in to theatre,' Sister Anne sympathised. 'Even if you offer to pay, you can't get such service any more. It's a shame. Admin ought to know that when remaining dressed for theatre you can hardly go along to the canteen.'

'Yes, I wonder how *they'd* like to go all day on just one meagre sandwich, without even a choice of filling!'

'I thought you'd be hungry.' Dr Seema Patel, the little Indian anaesthetist, appeared in the doorway at that moment, a paper bag in her hand. 'So I bought you this.'

'A Cornish pasty!' Rebecca exclaimed delightedly upon opening the bag and peering inside. 'You've just about saved my life, Seema!'

'If not her temper,' quipped Anne. 'Her tummy rumbles have kept us in fits for hours. They've been louder than the theatre machinery!'

'Yes, and very embarrassing they were, too.' Rebecca divided the pasty in two, offering one half to Anne.

'No, eat it all yourself, I'll get food at home.' Anne edged away.

John Barrie arrived that very instant, and from the way he eyed the pasty it was clear that he, too, had had nothing to eat for some time. Without a word, Rebecca passed him the half Anne had refused.

'Sure you can spare it?' He accepted it hungrily. 'The roads were so busy, it was impossible to stop for a snack anywhere.'

'Why, where've you been, Mr Barrie?' Anne asked.

'Culdrose,' Rebecca answered for him, before he could finish his mouthful of pasty and reply. Then, glancing at him, she read the warning in his eyes. So, she wasn't supposed to tell anyone about Selena's visit? But Geoffrey knew, so it wasn't all that much of a secret.

Then why should she be forced to keep secrets from Anne, who was becoming such a good friend? It would spoil things between them if she had to always be careful what she said. Once again her resentment against John started building up.

He had landed Selena on her without asking her permission and, while there had been no genuine 'thank you' from the girl herself, she would have expected some courtesy from him, some show of appreciation.

Instead, he was frowning at her, not smiling his gratitude. 'I'd hoped to find you busy in theatre,' he was saying rather sourly.

'I've already completed the repair of three hernias, Mr Barrie,' she replied with dignity.

'I'm now awaiting a four-year-old who's down for an appendicectomy. The delay is because he's had to have an X-ray, my houseman not being happy about the condition of the boy's chest.'

'Couldn't you have cleared out an abscess or two while waiting? The ops list is very long. It'll need our combined efforts if it's to be got through today.'

'Dr Shaw hasn't stopped working since she arrived in theatre, straight after finishing clinic,' Anne put in. 'But with you being away so long, there were some things none of us could get on with, Mr Barrie. We hadn't been told you wouldn't be coming in until after midday.' She spoke quite reprimandingly, adding, 'And now, at last, I'm off . . . it's *supposed* to be my half-day!' Pointedly, she glanced up at the clock.

Rebecca held her breath, waiting for the explosion. John was standing with arms folded, his face betraying some sort of battle going on inside him. Had Selena upset him? she wondered. Or was he merely unhappy at having had to part from her again? Whatever the trouble, Anne must certainly have added to it.

No one moved. It was like the lull before a storm. John looked at Rebecca, and from her to Anne; then, to everyone's surprise, he said, 'Judging from your faces, it seems I'm being unreasonable. Well, enjoy your late afternoon of freedom, Sister Campbell.' Then, touching Rebecca's elbow, 'Shall we get cracking now?' he suggested. 'There's a lot of work waiting.'

Finding his sudden change of mood quite mystifying, Rebecca walked beside him in silence. But soon she was too busy to think about anything but the little boy's welfare, and the abscesses she had to clear out after he had been seen to satisfactorily.

John came to her in theatre when she was clearing the fourth abscess on the list. 'Leave that one, Rebecca.' He still sounded amenable, although his face was as strained as before. 'Let your houseman take over, he needs the experience. I want you to assist at my next operation. A head injury.'

'Head injury? Isn't that a job for a neuro-surgeon?'

'There isn't one available, and it's an emergency.'

'What about Mr Hill? Shouldn't he be here?'

A frown settled back on John's face. 'You think I won't be able to cope?'

'No, but you'd be in serious trouble if anything went wrong. You're not being fair to yourself, taking on such a responsibility. One mistake and your career could be finished,' she reminded him. 'Besides, there's the patient to consider.'

'I am considering him!' John flared up, spoiling his earlier image. 'Don't you know I'm quite capable of reasoning out things for myself? Further delays might lose the man his life!'

No less worried, Rebecca secretly went to the phone while John was scrubbing up. She got through to Mr Hill, to whom she explained the situation and her fears.

He came along immediately but, taking her aside, he said quietly, 'You did the right thing in contacting me, but there was no need to worry on the patient's behalf—John held a neurosurgical post before coming here. Reports have it that he was very capable, which is just as well, as I'm a little out of practice in neurosurgery myself, not having had occasion to do any for quite a while.'

And he decided to let John play the major role in the operation, while he assisted.

Rebecca felt terrible. Her interference had proved unnecessary, as no doubt John would remind her in no uncertain terms afterwards. Besides, she had lost herself the chance to assist in an operation which would have provided valuable experience. Still, she comforted herself, she had acted in John's best interest—not that he was likely to agree!

With some trepidation, she faced him after the operation was successfully completed and Mr Hill had gone. But, when changed out of theatre gear and after writing up the theatre notes, John still had triumph in his eyes, and seemed disinclined to find fault with anything or anyone, for a change. 'Coming to the canteen?' he asked. 'We can allow ourselves a ten-minute break.'

'Mr Hill seemed pleased with the outcome of the operation?' she asked tentatively, to bring out into the open any grudge he might hold against her for calling Mr Hill to come and supervise.

'It went well.' John whistled between his teeth,

hurrying her along towards the canteen. 'I was glad he was there to observe and approve my technique,' he said with more than a touch of pride, after a moment or two. 'Now, you choose a table, and I'll do the fetching; it'll be quicker that way. You'll only deliberate over the choice of menu until there's no time left. I know how annoying females can be on these tight schedules.'

Vexed, Rebecca went to sit beside Seema. 'How's this arranged marriage of yours coming along?' she asked. 'I often wonder what would happen if you found you didn't like the young man your parents have selected.'

Seema smiled confidently. 'They would find someone more to my liking. They would not force me to marry a man I disliked. But it will not happen, they have chosen carefully. Kiran is a doctor; we shall have much in common. He is a good man.' She looked up as John approached with a loaded tray. 'Mr Barrie, he is a good man also. I would choose *him* as a husband for you, if I were your parents.' Then, collecting up her used dishes, she took them back to the counter.

'What did she say?' asked John, an unusual twinkle in his eye. 'Is she trying to pair us off?'

But Rebecca was more concerned with the fact that he had taken a dish of appetising hot-pot from the tray for himself, leaving her a salad.

'I wish I'd been offered a choice,' she said rebelliously. 'I'll need something more substantial than a salad if I'm to get through the rest of my on-duty time. Seema might be content to have choices made for her, but *I* come from a different culture, don't forget!'

'And that has something to do with hot-pot?' he asked, bemused.

'No. She's having an arranged marriage.' Watching him tucking in, Rebecca's mouth began to water, and her displeasure grew.

'Don't forget we only have ten minutes,' said John, rising. 'I'll get you some hot-pot, if that will satisfy you.' He came back with a steaming dish and a puzzled frown. 'I think I've got the hang of it,' he said. 'Dr Patel has had a marriage arranged for her, but you would prefer to choose for yourself?'

'No,' Rebecca sighed over his obtuseness. 'I simply wanted hot-pot, but wasn't given any option.'

'And you would prefer to choose your own husband?'

'Wouldn't you? If you were me, I mean.' She blew on her fork to cool down a piece of meat.

'I think we'd better concentrate on eating and getting back to theatre, before I become still further confused.' John sighed. 'Will you be long?'

Rebecca, still feeling rather abrasive, was too busy consuming both hot-pot and salad to have either the wish or the ability to reply. However, once she had finished eating, she trailed after him up the corridor, after taking his dishes and hers back to the counter.

'The kitchen staff object to collecting up dirty dishes,' she called out.

'But I didn't give them any choice in the matter?' John looked back at her. He clicked his tongue. 'Dear me,' he sighed, 'when will I ever learn?'

Rebecca laughed, suddenly seeing the funny side of the whole episode, and appreciating John being in a light-hearted mood again. Not that it lasted, which hardly surprised her—he seemed to fly off the handle more readily each day, as Anne verified.

'He's like a bear with a sore head,' she declared the following Saturday morning. 'The nurses are up in arms against him now, because he keeps telling them to be quiet even when they have something important to tell each other in theatre. What's troubling him, Rebecca? Is he aware that you're going out with Dr Dunn tonight? Could that be it?'

'No.' Rebecca tossed off the suggestion. 'He doesn't care what I do outside work.'

'Are you sure?' Anne gave her a questioning glance. 'We were hoping you might have some influence over him. Someone ought to speak up for the nurses. He's always been so courteous towards them until now. I'm sure he doesn't realise how extra difficult he's become. Well, I'd better get back to the hospital. I only ran over to see if there's anything you could do to alleviate matters.'

'If the opportunity crops up, I'll try,' Rebecca

promised. 'But I can't guarantee success. He doesn't seem any better pleased with me than with the rest of theatre staff, especially just lately. I simply irritate him.'

'I have my own opinion about that,' Anne said with a knowing look. Then she left Rebecca to get on with the studying she was wanting to finish before getting ready for the evening.

As the minutes ticked by, she became more and more loath to keep the date with Geoffrey. Why she had ever agreed to go out with him she now failed to understand. Even when relaxing in the fragrance of her bath, into which she had poured whatever residue of her bath oils Selena had left, she remained anxious and annoyed with herself for not refusing his invitation.

Even dressing up for the occasion became a chore. The prospect of wearing the treasured evening dress no longer gave her any pleasure. Nevertheless, she talcumed and scented herself in an effort to make herself feel special, hoping that would help her enjoy the evening in some small way.

Having made up her face, she slipped into the dress, smoothing it down over her pure silk lingerie, then surveyed her reflection in the full-length mirror. Her slender figure was shown off to perfection by the black sophistication of the slim-fitting dress, while her hair, when brushed and swept to one side, was truly glorious in its various shades of gold and amber, bronze and copper.

For a wistful instant she wished John could see her looking her best, instead of the way she had to look when in theatre with her hair pushed out of sight, her feet in men's size clogs, and the over-long green gown bulked out by theatre trouser-suits which fitted only where they touched.

Even when not in theatre gear, any smart dress she wore would necessarily be hidden under a grimy white coat, its over-full pockets crammed with stethoscope and a dozen other medical necessities. It was no wonder he found her irritating!

She paused in her thoughts, wondering why it was John she was thinking of, not Richard. But, of course, Richard would still carry a picture of her as an exuberant, fun-loving medic, whereas she had become a staid, dedicated surgeon. At least, that was how she saw herself. Three years had made a big difference to her life. How had time dealt with him? One day she would pluck up the courage to ask John.

There was a knock on the door when she was changing her ear-rings from pearl studs to long jet drops.

'Dramatic, my fiery-haired beauty,' Geoffrey declared, studying her as she opened the door, the hall-light making a glowing background. 'You'll be a sensation!'

'Newquay,' he said, bowing her into his red sports car, 'that's where we're going, celebrating the world surfing championships. I'm a part-time instructor myself, I might even teach you to surf, one day.'

They stopped at a fine hotel overlooking the sands and the big breakers. Rebecca quite enjoyed meeting other members of the surfing club, although Geoffrey tended to whisk her away after a few words of greeting, seemingly intent on introducing her to as many people as possible.

'Well, I'm proud of you,' was his excuse, when she eventually protested that her feet were killing her and she needed to sit down. 'I want to show you off, not hide you away in some corner!'

'I'm afraid flattery doesn't make high-heeled sandals any the more comfortable,' Rebecca countered. 'And I'm getting embarrassed by the many people who keep asking you to bring me along to various social activities. I don't get time to explain I've a Fellowship to gain, and many long hard-working weeks to get through.'

'I know you have, darling, and it's a shame,' he replied with mock sympathy. 'But I told you that you ought to get married and not bother your beautiful head about the more mundane things in life.'

'What's that?' asked one of his sporting friends, edging nearer. 'Are you two talking marriage?' He winked at Rebecca. 'Geoff's a lucky man; I'm partial to redheads myself. Invite me to the wedding, won't you, old boy?' Then he wandered away again.

'Champagne's gone to his head,' said Geoffrey. 'I think it must be going to my head too, because the idea he's put there is tempting me. I could do with a wife—not that I'm in any hurry to settle down——'

'Well, I'm in a hurry to get back to my flat. Have you seen the time?' Rebecca tapped his wrist-watch. 'I'm on early tomorrow, so I must get in a few hours' sleep.'

'One more drink,' insisted Geoffrey. 'What'll you have?'

'Nothing, and I don't think you should have any more. You're driving, remember—unless you'd like me to?'

'What, have a female drive my jalopy?' He was scandalised, and showed it, but her words did stop him from drinking any more before they left. Fortunately he had sufficient control over himself not to drink before working in theatre—no one could accuse him of irresponsibility in that respect—but outside the hours of work he was quite likely to over-indulge his liking for alcohol.

'Oh, please drive more carefully,' she implored time and time again when on the way back to the hospital, until, losing patience, he stopped by the side of the road.

'Are you sore because there wasn't a slap-up meal?' he asked sulkily. 'I didn't mislead you deliberately about that. We were too late for the dinner, the drive there took longer than I planned. Blame the traffic, not me.'

'I'm not bothered about the dinner, I just don't think you should be driving, the state you're in.'

'State?' He put his arm around her. 'State of

unappeased desire, is that what you mean? Give me a kiss, then, Rebecca.' He ran a hand through her hair, loosening it so that it spread out about her shoulders. 'Show me you care, and I'll drive like a Grand Prix champion!'

'Just drive safely, that's all I ask.' Rebecca pushed him away.

'A kiss first, to fuel me on my way,' he demanded.

Resisting, Rebecca sought a way to escape. A long, deserted road stretched ahead, fields on either side shrouded in a white evening mist. Bitterly regretting being with Geoffrey, she thought hard, eventually devising a plan which she hoped would thwart him.

Managing to persuade him to drive on by suggesting that a proper lay-by would give them more privacy, she jumped out as soon as the car stopped, knowing of a pedestrians-only path which led from that lay-by to the hospital residences. Then she picked up her long skirt and ran.

For a moment or two Geoffrey called after her to come back. She made no attempt to answer, and carefully kept herself hidden in the shadows cast by the high hedges and overhanging trees, knowing that he would be reluctant to leave his car unattended in order to seek her out—also that he would soon stop calling, being near enough to the accommodation flats to be heard. He would hardly relish having the news blazoned around that he'd been deserted by a girl!

The rough path was squelchy with mud from recent rain. Rebecca soon lost one of her sandals. She hopped around on one foot, trying to find it. Unsuccessful, she took off the other sandal and, carrying it, ran to her flat. Only when the curtains were drawn and the door locked did she feel at ease. She could well imagine Geoffrey reacting aggressively after being treated so summarily, especially when labouring under the influence of too much wine.

Filling a large bowl with warm water and fetching a towel, she sat down to bathe her feet, not bothering to remove her tights first. They were ruined anyway. She grimaced at the ladders running here, there and everywhere. Her best tights, too!

There was a knock on her front door.

'Who's there?' she called, determined not to open to Geoffrey, but rather hoping it might be Anne popping in after a Saturday night disco.

'Just me,' answered John Barrie.

What could he want? Curious to find out, Rebecca wrapped a towel around her soaking wet feet, and did a series of sack-race jumps to the front door, then endeavoured to turn and hop back to the lounge, John close behind her. The towel making things difficult, she tripped, and was saved from an undignified fall only by the swiftness of John's reaction.

An arm shooting out to encircle her waist, he swung her across his left hip and held her there until he could safely put her down on the chair beside the bowl. He looked down at the water. 'Corns?' he suggested, amused.

'No!' she denied indignantly.

'You're giving your feet a mud-bath to improve their complexion? Shouldn't you have taken your tights off first?'

She glowered at him. 'I've simply been out jogging,' she said.

'In that dress, and through mud?' His blue eyes filled with scepticism.

'Why have you come?' she asked, annoyed to have him see her in such disarray. 'I wasn't expecting visitors—not at this time of night, anyhow.' She frowned disapprovingly.

John's expression sobered. 'Geoffrey Dunn returned alone. Shut himself into his room before I could get a word out of him. I was concerned for your welfare, but now——' Pointedly he glanced down at the bowl of muddied water. 'I can guess what happened.'

'It really isn't any business of yours,' Rebecca returned icily.

'Very well. As long as you're all right, I'll say goodnight and go.' Then John noticed the mud stains on the carpet in the lounge and hall. 'The cleaners won't be very pleased when they see this mess,' he remarked. 'I'll clean it up for you. You're not dressed for domestic work.'

Rebecca was too amazed to do anything but stare as he brought a pail, scrubbing brush and detergent from the kitchen, and, on his hands and knees, attacked the unsightly brown patches.

'Well, that's done.' He came out of the kitchen, drying his hands after he had finished. 'Let's hope the wetness dries off by the morning without leaving the carpet too mottled.'

'Thank you,' Rebecca said, looking up at him.

Swiftly he bent and kissed her lightly on her surprised lips. 'It was nice having you tucked safely under my arm,' he remarked, then left the flat.

Rebecca ran the tip of her pink tongue around her mouth, almost as if she expected to find traces of the kiss still there.

Then she saddened, remembering Selena's existence.

CHAPTER EIGHT

AWAKENED by her alarm clock at seven the next morning, Rebecca hurried to dress, make tea, eat a small helping of muesli, then rush across to the hospital, calling in at the little Catholic chapel where the Blessed Sacrament was reserved. There she flopped down on to her knees and begged for help not to make any more stupid mistakes . . . especially not when working with John Barrie, she added fervently.

Upon coming out, she almost bumped into him. Looking to see where she had been, he nodded. 'While you're about it, add a prayer for Veronica Main,' he suggested, falling into step beside her.

'Veronica Main?' The name was unfamiliar to her.

'Yes, we're operating on her this morning. We have to take some of her brain away.' His expression was grave, and his manner completely formal. The kiss of the night before might never have been, Rebecca reflected, finding herself even wondering whether she might have dreamt it. Then his words began to sink in.

'Take part of her brain away?' she echoed, horrified. 'Oh, poor girl! Whatever happened?'

'Road accident. A drunken driver lost control of

his car and crossed lanes, crashing into Veronica's Mini. Part of her head was crushed beyond repair. Goodness knows how she'll be affected—change of personality, loss of faculties, inability to cope? We just can't say. She's only twenty-three. A mother of two. It really is tragic.'

There was nothing Rebecca could say, she shared his apprehension on Veronica's behalf so completely.

'Geoffrey Dunn is listed as the anaesthetist for the operation,' John went on. 'I hope he learns a lesson from it. I'm to assist as second surgeon, which means you'll be having to deal with an emergency by yourself. Your particular patient came in about an hour ago with an acutely tender, reddened swelling over the top of his leg——'

'Strangulated femoral hernia?' suggested Rebecca.

'Correct. Think you can manage on your own?'

'Yes.' She made herself sound more confident than she felt right at that moment.

'Good. And don't forget to talk your houseman through the operation so that he can learn while watching and assisting.'

Scrubbed and ready, Tim beside her and Sister Anne standing by with a scrub nurse, Rebecca took over the anaesthetised patient, making a transverse incision over the swelling.

'The hernia sac will be lying directly under the skin and subcutaneous fat,' she told Tim, 'so we incise the sac, inspect the part of the bowel that's contained in the hernia—you can expect it to look a rather dusky blue—then we dissect the sac down to the hernia neck, which is the femoral canal, of course. Have you got all that?'

Busy holding the retractors in position, Tim smiled his appreciation of her detailed teaching. 'I think so,' he said, although still seeming a little lost.

Continuing, Rebecca displayed the neck of the hernia, eased it, and enlarged it slightly, so that the bowel was not so strangulated. 'That's to improve the blood supply,' she informed Tim. Then, asking the nurse for some hot 'wet packs', she placed them over the bowel and left them for five minutes to see whether the bowel pinked up again.

Conscious of the large figure coming into theatre, she glanced up. John Barrie was standing watching. She showed him the bowel, which was already looking pink and healthy again. 'It's showing peristaltic movements,' she pointed out, as much for Tim's enlightenment as anything.

'Yes, it looks viable,' John agreed, staying while she returned it through the hernia orifice back into the abdomen. Then he left.

She knew why he had come from the theatre where he was working in order to check up on her progress. The strangulated bit of bowel could become gangrenous if not seen to straight away, which would mean a larger operation involving going into the abdomen, resecting the gangrenous portion of bowel and joining up the two ends of bowel . . . in which case he would have to do the operation himself, or at least supervise.

'He's a dedicated surgeon,' she found herself remarking to Tim. 'Really cares about the patients, and takes endless trouble to make sure everything possible is done to help them.'

'A bit formidable, though,' Tim replied. 'I wouldn't like to get on the wrong side of him!'

'No, well, he's a perfectionist and something of a workaholic, and expects his juniors to be the same.' As I know to my cost, she could have added, although she resisted the temptation. Even mentioning John Barrie was becoming difficult, her feelings about him remaining so raw and vulnerable, and quite beyond her understanding.

'I never thought surgery would impress me so much,' Tim said reflectively. 'But when clerking in patients and hearing of the suffering they've been enduring, I've realised it must be a great consolation to be able to do something to alleviate their pain.'

'Yes,' agreed Rebecca, 'I always think that the pain they come in with is sure to get worse, whereas the pain we send them home with *should* soon get better.'

'If this patient here had had a spinal anaesthetic plus some sedative, what would have been the procedure then?' asked Tim, as she trimmed the hernia sac, stitching its base, then popped it back through the femoral canal.

'We'd have had to wait twenty minutes after

the anaesthetic was put in, and a nurse would have stayed talking to the patient while he was awake, to take his mind off what was happening.' Rebecca was closing the defect with strong non-absorbable sutures as she talked. Then, signalling for the scrub nurse to give Tim the skin suture, she showed him how to close the skin.

'Now the patient goes into the recovery area for about twenty minutes, before being returned to the ward,' she said when he'd completed the job to her satisfaction. 'And we can have a cup of coffee while we write up the operation notes. Your name will appear on them as well as mine.'

'And I'll be on my way to becoming a bona-fide surgeon?' Tim beamed.

Rebecca knew just how he felt. She was still filled with the same sort of enthusiasm for the job.

Anne had already organised coffee for the theatre staff, but it was a relief to everyone when Geoffrey Dunn failed to appear. As far as Rebecca was concerned, she would have liked nothing better than never to have to see him again. And he, she imagined, felt pretty much the same about her.

The rest of the day was hectic, one operation following another.

'How will we know if that strangulated hernia op was successful?' Tim queried anxiously, before he left to clerk in some of the newly arrived surgical patients who were being settled into various wards.

'If peritonitis doesn't set in over the next twenty-four to thirty-six hours,' Rebecca answered, tensing a little, not liking to even think about such a possibility. Hastily, she turned her mind to the next operation on the list, a haemorrhoidectomy.

Later, after dealing with an abnormal appendix, followed by ligation of varicose veins and several minor ops under local anaesthetic, such as excising warts, sebaceous cysts and ingrowing toenails, she found that John Barrie was free to do the laparotomy on the list and expected her to assist.

By this time it was after two o'clock and she had had nothing to eat or drink, except for the cup of coffee, since her meagre breakfast. Whether or not John had stopped for a meal she had no idea, except that she knew he rarely bothered with food when there was a list to get through.

To complain that she was hungry would have been asking for trouble. All the same, she felt a little faint for want of some sort of sustenance.

The laparotomy led to the discovery that there was an aortic aneurism to be repaired, so Rebecca was in theatre most of the afternoon, which left her feeling like a wet rag and, she thought, quite incapable of standing up to anyone, especially John Barrie.

However, he proved as demanding as ever, so it was a great relief when it was possible to break away to the changing-room.

Anaesthetist Seema Patel had taken over from Geoffrey Dunn for the laparotomy. She came in to share the changing-room with Rebecca.

'When's the wedding to be?' asked Rebecca, less out of curiosity than a wish to relax her mind by dwelling on something outside surgery and medicine.

'Everyone is asking me,' sighed Seema. 'I am so embarrassed because I cannot answer. I must wait until I see Kiran.' At his name her cheeks reddened. 'He might not like me enough to marry me.' She covered her face with her slender hands. 'At this moment, and on other such moments, I would wish to be an animal,' she continued softly. 'Animals do not blush!'

Rebecca touched her lightly on the arm. 'I'm sorry if I embarrassed you, Seema. Please forgive me. I won't ask any awkward questions again. It was thoughtless of me.'

'Oh, no, no, you are my friend.' Seema's glowing brown eyes warmed to her. 'I do not mind what *you* ask. It is my cheeks which do not behave as they should.'

'Will you go back to India with Kiran?' Rebecca hoped she was not again embarrassing Seema, but fortunately she took the question in her stride without becoming at all disconcerted.

'For a short time—that is, if we do marry, but he is trying to get a post in a British hospital so that we could stay over here where he could sit for his Fellowship exams. Yet, if so many wards are to be closed countrywide, not so many doctors will be employed, and his chances of working here will be limited.' Anxiety lines deepened across the normally smooth forehead.

'You would prefer to stay here?'

'Oh, yes, although one day I will go back and help my own people. It is essential we train over here first, to gain experience and the necessary qualifications. Kiran wants to do that, but with all the cutbacks in the Health Service, will he be given a job? That is our worry.'

'I hope he will,' Rebecca said, as she finished dressing. 'Our consultants might be able to help. Come to the canteen and let's talk about it. I'm starving!'

'Please, you will excuse me, but I must write to my family. They expect a letter each week.'

'See you later, then.' Rebecca went off on her own. The canteen was crowded with nurses having supper. About to join them, she was stopped by a touch on her arm. Immediately her blood raced. Without checking, she knew that John was at her elbow.

'This way, not that.' Imperiously he steered her towards the door.

She pulled away. 'I must get something to eat,' she insisted, doing her level best to ignore the effect his unexpected presence was having on her heart.

'Don't make a scene, dozens of eyes are watching. I merely want you to come to the office for a moment.' His voice was low and unsettlingly husky, not at all stern and commanding as when in theatre. His hand still rested on her arm, and something about his touch made her want to close her eyes to the world and lean against him just to feel his nearness. Nevertheless, she steeled herself against the attraction he engendered. He was so like Richard that he stirred up the romantic feelings she had once known—that was all there was to it, she assured herself. It certainly was not that he appealed to her in the way Richard had. No, of course not. He simply reminded her of the happy, carefree days when she and his cousin had been so much in love.

Richard had been free at the time, too, whereas from what Geoffrey had hinted, John had, or would soon have, a wife to consider—a wife who could well be the very demanding Selena. Rebecca was sure Richard would have had more sense than to fall for someone like Selena . . .

Drawing herself up, she again pulled away from the proprietary hand on her arm.

'Please come,' John urged, and, although she hesitated, she finally followed him. He closed the door of the office behind her.

'We've had a very uncompromising answer to our letters of protest,' he began. 'The consultants have it at the moment, but they've suggested we write a follow-up letter to our first.' He looked down at what was presumably a rough draft lying on his desk. 'We must point out that, although closing Ward Eight might save money, it also cuts down on the number of patients we can admit. Also that with the patients having to have increased sick-leave in many cases, because of the lengthening waiting lists, that might mean more expensive treatment becoming necessary by the time they do eventually come into hospital . . . with the result that the taxpayers lose out once again, the closure costing them more, even if the money comes from a different pocket.'

'Yes, I see what you mean. There's an eroding of goodwill between patients and NHS doctors and nurses, too. We doctors still expect nurses to look after our patients satisfactorily, even when they're deprived of sufficient personnel and facilities, and of course the patients resent the long waits, and grumble at the nurses, who in their turn blame us!'

'Obviously you've cottoned on to the general idea.' John pushed blank sheets of paper across the desk towards her. 'Well, get busy, I'm told you can type. There's a machine over there. You seemed keen to help earlier on.'

Rebecca stared, too stunned to speak.

'You know,' John continued, ignoring her lack of response, 'thirty years ago there was only one administrative officer here, and one radiologist. Now there are a hundred on the Admin staff, yet *still* only one radiologist! That speaks for itself, doesn't it?'

Rebecca had stopped listening. 'Are you seriously expecting *me* to compose the follow-up letter and type it out?' She could hardly believe it.

'Of course. What do you think I brought you along here for? And when the finished product is approved, get all the junior doctors to sign again, and use all the charm you possess to include consultants, nursing staff and—yes, I think this is a good idea—you could also include any patients willing to add their names.'

'You really want me to put my career at risk by getting known as a trouble-maker?' Rebecca's rising anger left her hot and highly indignant. What was happening was quite incredible—she could hardly believe John had meant what he had said, although his expression had been serious enough.

He turned when about to go through the doorway. 'You could, of course, add a claim for worn-out shoe leather because of all the miles you trudge along corridors looking for our patients, now they've been moved into other wards. Use any compensation you're given to fund a decent pair of shoes—yours squeak abominably in the dead of night when the patients are trying to sleep.'

'Oh!' gasped Rebecca, unable to find words capable of expressing her feelings.

'And,' John came back to poke his head around the doorpost, 'recalling the sandals you ruined when jogging through mud the other night, make the letter strong, then you might get enough to pay for another pair!'

He *can't* be serious, Rebecca assured herself,

and called down the corridor after his fast
receding figure, 'I don't intend writing the letter,
Mr Barrie!'

He took no notice.

'I'm hungry!' she added as a last appeal.

Turning, he put a silencing finger to his lips,
then continued on his way.

Rebecca remained where she stood for a few
more seconds, her exasperation growing. Then,
defiantly banging the door of the office after her,
she hurried back to the canteen.

CHAPTER NINE

AFTER collecting a steak and kidney pie and chips from the counter, Rebecca was again about to join a group of nurses at one of the tables, but changed her mind and sat alone instead, wanting to think.

Surprising even herself, her mind was still on the letter she was supposed to write. Drawing a couple of paper serviettes towards her, she made notes, framing sentences this way, then that. But why am I wasting time doing this? she asked herself, knowing she had no intention of doing John Barrie's work for him. If he wanted the letter written, he would have to write it himself, she muttered inwardly. What a nerve, passing the job on the way he had! Nevertheless, in spite of her resentment, gradually the letter took shape, almost as if composing itself. The pie and chips, meanwhile, grew greasily colder and colder.

'I thought you were hungry.' At the sound of John's voice, she quickly snatched up the serviettes and crumpled them into one of the large pockets of her white coat.

John took the seat beside her and eyed her plate. 'I can never understand why some people buy hot food, then let it grow cold,' he remarked.

She sat perfectly still, making no attempt to reply.

'Would a good dinner loosen your tongue?' Again that touch of humour in his voice. Did he take her seriously only when they were working together?

'I'll stand you a decent meal one night, if you care to come,' he added quietly, moving his chair closer to hers.

She agonised over the invitation, longing to accept. Her conscience intervened, however, reminding her that Selena was the one he should take out if company was what he wanted. After all, he could be with her within an hour.

Very much on her dignity, she stood up. 'You'll excuse me, Mr Barrie,' she said over-politely, 'but my time is fully occupied. I have an exam to study for, and other important things to do.'

'Such as a letter to write?' he called after her as she walked away.

Her eyes downcast, she almost bumped into Geoffrey Dunn.

'Oh, hello.' He glanced from her through the glass-panelled door to where John was sitting. 'You had our dear registrar's company at table, did you? He looks rather lost—as if you've just deserted him. Was it his fault you left your food untouched?'

'You were spying!' She sounded outraged.

'Not really, I just happened to see.' He gave her a calculating look. 'I've forgiven you, you know. It took me a time, but I came to it in the end. So now, to show an equally good will, what about dining with me? Or do you prefer to hold grudges?'

Ill at ease, and still resenting John's attitude over the letter, Rebecca hesitated. Her hand crept into her coat pocket, fingering the serviettes. She crumpled them up still further. No one was more against the closure of Ward Eight than she was, but there were others who could put the arguments, who *should* do so. The onus should not be laid solely on her shoulders. For all she knew, she was being made use of. John Barrie was quite capable of fighting his own battles . . . anyone would think she had all the spare time in the world! Fancy expecting her to chase around collecting signatures again!

Her mind ran round in circles, indignation mounting. Just because she had won those four extra beds that time! Well, that had been *her* part of the protest, now someone else could and should take over. It was up to John Barrie to try a little diplomacy instead of veiled threats, then perhaps Admin might soften too.

She dropped the serviettes into a nearby waste-bin. 'All right,' she said to Geoffrey. 'I'll eat with you, but not outside the hospital. In the canteen or nowhere.'

He sighed, and was about to object when suddenly he brightened instead. 'Let's sit at John's table,' he suggested mischievously. 'I want to see his face when he realises you're with me.'

'You *what*?' Positively oozing anger, Rebecca turned and walked away, refusing to return, even when Geoffrey tried to convince her he had been joking.

'I'm not being made a means of revenge,' she snapped. 'Nor am I prepared to be anybody's tool, not yours, not John's——' And not Richard's, her mind added, although she made no mention of his name out loud. 'I'm my own person, and intend to stay that way!'

From that moment on she became something of a loner outside work, disappearing into her flat to study as soon as she was off duty. Anne and Seema were the only visitors she welcomed. It was as if John and Geoffrey had been struck off her social list, although, when working with them, she was as co-operative as with the other doctors.

Not that John seemed to think so. Appearing more than a little put out, he tackled her about her changed attitude, just when she had more or less accepted that he had completely lost interest in her.

'I thought we were becoming friends, perhaps even more than friends,' he said one day, when finding her on her own in the doctors' rest-room. 'But somehow things seem to have gone sour. Why, Rebecca? Do you know?'

She took a quick peep at his stern face. His deep-set eyes had a vexed and quizzical look, his well-shaped lips were narrowed into a thin line. Inflexible as he was, there was still an attractiveness there to which she felt herself yielding, an appeal that was too strong to ignore.

'I don't know what you mean.' She stalled for time to think up some feasible excuses, well aware that she had been deliberately avoiding him, purposely trying to dodge the possibility of disconcerting tête-à-têtes. Not that she disliked being alone with him, she reminded herself with her usual honesty, she was simply scared, frightened of the feelings he could arouse so easily. It was his cousin she loved, she must never forget that.

And he, for his part, was emotionally involved with Selena, if what Geoffrey had said was true. Geoffrey was not given to spreading scandal usually, not when sober anyway, and in full control of himself.

John stood waiting, a picture of arrogance and strength. He was obviously determined to get a straight answer from her.

'All right,' she looked up at him fearlessly, steeling her heart against him, 'if you want to know, you're proving to be a distraction, just when I'm wanting to concentrate on building up a career in surgery.'

Turning his back for a moment, he lowered his proud head and his shoulders shook.

'You're laughing at me!' Rebecca cried indignantly. 'I can tell you it's no joke trying to master the academics of the job when romance is rearing its ugly head wherever one looks and whatever one does!'

He laughed outright at that, turning to her again. 'I've never heard romance described in quite those terms before. Oh, Rebecca, you're a gem!' Putting both hands on her shoulders he drew her to him. 'You know, I believe you're as attracted to me as I am to you. You try to pretend it's because you see Richard in me, but you know as well as I do that there's more to it than that. There's a magic in the air whenever our hands touch, an excitement in being close, even when at an operating-table. In fact, when you look across at me sometimes, I could swear your eyes are kissing me!'

'You've no business to imagine such things . . . no right to suppose emotions that shouldn't be there!' Rebecca's green eyes grew increasingly misty. 'I wish you'd never come to this hospital . . . Oh, why don't you leave me alone?' She blinked hard and furiously.

'Alone to dream fantasies around cousin Richard?' John's arms dropped aimlessly to his sides. 'When *will* this nonsense cease?' His voice had a sharp edge to it, and the eyes he turned on her were icily cold. 'You've put Richard up on a pedestal, pretending he'll develop the character and nature you've wished on him. Had you really loved him, you would have accepted him as he was, warts and all! Instead, you presumed you could mould him to your own design. It's been that way all along, only you won't allow yourself to realise it. Svengali in reverse, I call it!'

His knuckles showed white as he clenched his

fists before pushing them well down into his trouser pockets.

Rebecca's eyes were dry and hard again, and a very dark green.

'I don't like talking to you like this, but someone has to, Rebecca.' John seemed to have to force himself to continue. 'You stand to ruin your chances of happiness, and all because of a false sense of loyalty to someone who quite possibly has no use for that loyalty, not wanting it.'

She swallowed hard and walked to the door. 'I'm going up to see my patients, Mr Barrie. At least *they* want me.'

As if she had heard her, Mrs Peters, a large lady in the first bed she visited, greeted her warmly, raising her spirits a little. 'Haven't been as comfortable as this for weeks, Doc,' she beamed. 'What's in this cushion I'm sitting on, water or sponge?'

'Silicon gel, that's why it's nicknamed a jelly cushion.'

'Ask a silly question . . .' laughed Mrs Peters. Then she went on to say, 'But it's not just the cushion I've to thank, it's *you*, for the good job you made of my haemorrhoids.'

Rebecca smiled her appreciation, then walked on to see Mrs Taylor, an eighty-four-year-old who lay in a corner with her face to the wall. Reports had it that she had given up the will to live, her husband having died from a stroke just a few days before she herself was admitted to hospital. Since then she had refused to speak to anyone.

Sitting on the side of her bed, Rebecca caught hold of the care-worn hand and stroked it sympathetically. Mrs Taylor turned slightly, her chin quivering. 'It would've been our jubilee next week,' she half sobbed aloud.

'Only queens have jubilees!' the patient in the next bed remonstrated.

'Nonsense!' Mrs Taylor turned more fully to face the speaker. 'Anyone can have jubilees if they live long enough . . .'

'Which is like saying the older you are, the less likely you are to die young,' returned another neighbour tauntingly.

Rebecca spun round disapprovingly, only to be met by a knowing wink, making her realise that Mrs Taylor was being intentionally goaded into retaliation. And it was working! Already she was raising herself up against her pillow, the spark of battle animating her faded blue eyes. Nodding encouragement and thanks to the well-meaning goaders, Rebecca slipped away, glad because Mrs Taylor had been drawn out of her grief and misery and was being given something of a zest for life again. Ordinary people without any special training were doing more for the old lady than any doctor or medicine. It was a very humbling thought!

Patients and their problems had completely absorbed her until John Barrie had arrived on the scene, she reflected ruefully, wishing she could return to the halcyon days when she had been so sure Richard would eventually become the person she wanted him to be. She had been quite content to wait, losing herself in her work and furthering her career.

But John had disturbed the equilibrium of her life, had replaced certainty with doubts, and had somehow made himself become important to her, in more ways than one. She was constantly having to battle with her heart whenever he came near, so was still doing her best to avoid him. It was a relief when he went away for a few days to attend a conference.

A relief, yet the hospital suddenly seemed very empty without him. It was surprising how the time seemed to drag, in spite of the extra effort she was putting into getting to know the patients, their families and their needs.

'It's all too easy to visit them just before their ops, then give them another quick check afterwards, without really becoming acquainted with them,' she said to Tim one day, when they were walking through the wards. 'One could easily become a robot doctor that way. I've been guilty in that respect myself just lately, my mind being on other things.'

'Such as Mr Barrie?' Tim gave her an astute glance. 'He isn't easy to ignore, is he?'

'Oh, look!' Embarrassed, Rebecca halted outside the sister's office. 'Here's Sister Anne. I just want to have a word with her. You can go on, and I'll meet you on Ward Twelve in a few minutes.'

Anne looked up from her paper work. 'What d'you think?' she began. 'We've been told not to order any more stationery for three months! Isn't that just about the limit? Admin's clamping down on everything. Anyhow, I thought that instead of just sitting moaning, we'd raise some extra cash ourselves.' She eyed the sheet of paper lying apart from the various medical forms. 'The first thing on the agenda is a sponsored walk.'

'To where?'

'We'll do one of the Coombe Valley nature trails.'

'What, way up near Bude?' Rebecca shook a doubtful head.

'I know what you're thinking.' Anne chewed the end of her pencil and looked up at the ceiling as if for inspiration. 'You'll need transport to get there. Well, I'll fix you up somehow.'

An invasion of nurses called for her attention. 'I'll work on the sponsorship idea tonight,' she said, putting the paper away. 'My long-suffering husband can organise things. It'll help keep him awake, otherwise I'll be the usual TV widow. That man of mine's mesmerised by the box. Lounges in front of it, slumbering like a baby, yet as soon as I try to change the channel he's wide awake, asking "why". "I was watching that!" he'll claim, aggrieved. It's funny how men hate admitting they've been dozing, isn't it? Don't ever marry one, Dr Shaw, they're the laziest creatures on earth. I don't know why we love 'em, do you?'

The nurses all laughed, but Rebecca merely smiled wryly as she left the office to meet up with her houseman. Would she ever have a husband? she wondered, then put the thought from her, not wanting to let her mind travel down that particular road again.

Finding Tim, she left him again almost at once, when she realised she was due to do the varicose vein operation on Mr Hill's list. He had asked her to do this last one of the day in his stead, so that he could attend the surgical division meeting in Truro. Knowing she had no time to waste, because not enough nurses were on late duty to cover any but emergency operations after five o'clock, yet finding the patient wouldn't be ready until half-past four, Rebecca was more than a little put out, especially when she found that Geoffrey was to be the anaesthetist.

He was in his most provoking mood, criticising unmercifully. 'Your hand's trembling,' he insisted time and time again, making it more difficult for her to keep it steady, just when she was making small incisions over the worst of the varicose veins, carefully following the lines Mr Hill had marked on the skin with his felt-tipped pen.

'And as registrar John isn't here to upset you emotionally,' Geoffrey said in his taunting way, 'could it be that *I'm* the one you're desiring?'

'Please be quiet, Dr Dunn, you're flustering me!' Rebecca rebuked him sharply, inadvertently dropping one of the clips to the floor while dissecting out a deep perforating vein. Then, as she reached out to the scrub nurse for a replacement clip, her theatre cap slipped forward, almost covering her eyes.

Calling to another nurse to adjust the cap, because neither she nor the scrub nurse could touch it as it was unsterile, she found herself the butt of Geoffrey's most ribald humour. Ignoring his attempts to rile her called for much self-restraint, so it was a great relief when the operation was over and she and the nursing team could get away.

'I'm to be in Culdrose shortly,' Geoffrey called after Rebecca, making her blood run cold. She was so sure that in the mood he was in he must be planning some mischief, and equally sure that, if so, John Barrie would be his target.

'I think Mr Dunn is suffering from unrequited love,' remarked the scrub nurse when in the changing-room. 'I'm sure he fancies you, Dr Shaw.'

'Then he has a very funny way of showing it,' Rebecca replied drily. She was worried. His mention of Culdrose had implied to her a meeting with Selena. Alarmed on John's behalf, she decided to stay behind after writing up her operation notes and confront Geoffrey, asking straight out why he was going to Culdrose. Greater than the desire to keep away from him was the need she felt to save John from unnecessary hurt.

She looked for him, but he was still with the

patient; then, when the patient was being taken back to the ward, Geoffrey disappeared before she could get hold of him.

John returned from his conference, and it seemed to her that he was more remote than usual, as if he had something other than work on his mind. From the looks he kept giving her, she felt she must in some way be connected with his preoccupation; nevertheless, she still avoided him as much as possible and tried to throw herself heart and soul into her work.

Finally the day of the sponsored walk arrived.

'I've fixed you up with transport,' Anne told her.

'Not with Anaesthetist Dunn, I hope?'

'No, I don't even know if he's coming. He hasn't been seen lately. Mr Barrie's taking you. He offered, so I thought you two could make up a couple—everyone else has a partner.'

Still concerned over Geoffrey's absence, wondering whether he was still in Culdrose and, if so, why, Rebecca failed to take in Anne's words at first, but when they did sink in she clapped a hand to her mouth, aghast. 'Oh, Anne, not Mr Barrie! Did you have to? I've been trying to avoid him lately.'

'He offered,' Anne said nonchalantly, 'and you needed the transport.'

'I don't have to stay with him all day, do I?' Rebecca seemed quite distressed.

'No, of course not, just join up with any of the others once you get to Bude.' Anne frowned, puzzled. 'I didn't know you disliked him all that much,' she added.

Rebecca was silent. It would have been nice to be able to confide the whole story to Anne, she thought wistfully, but how could she? John's marriage was his secret, it was not up to her to betray it.

'It's wonderful the way duties have been covered so willingly by those who can't take part, and the way sponsorship promises have poured in,' Anne said, going back to checking her lists of participants in the walk.

'I had to rely on patients and staff to sponsor me,' Rebecca remarked a little sadly. 'I don't know many people outside the hospital—I never get time to do much socialising.'

'Whereas I have family all over Cornwall, so I was able to bludgeon them and their friends into contributing. They all hate the sight of me now, and hide when they see me coming, but I don't care as long as they pay up!' Anne gave a carefree laugh.

Not really listening, Rebecca was busy working out whether there would be time for her to go to her flat and change into something more fetching than the old sweater and jeans she had put on ready to go scrambling over rough ground in the valley. Would John think her very untidy, unattractively so? He was always so immaculate himself.

Even while admonishing herself for still wanting him to find her appealing, she looked for an opportunity to rush away and dress up a little, but he came in to make up her mind for her by immediately catching hold of her arm and urging her along. He looked down at her. 'There, did you feel it?' he asked, raising his eyebrows. 'That electricity I told you about, did it fire you as it fired me?' Then, as if what he had said was of no consequence, he went on, 'Everyone's outside, raring to go. Come on, what's holding you back?'

Her emotions all at sixes and sevens, she ran with him—she had to, he kept such a tight grip on her wrist. Then, helping her into his car, he fastened the seat-belt around her and actually smiled in a relaxed, happy way.

Watching him as he started up the engine, she found herself melting towards him and, in spite of niggling qualms, her sense of excitement grew, but taking her feelings in hand she quietened them down deliberately. Only unhappiness lay in John's direction, she reminded herself, so the only thing to do was battle against him in every way she could.

CHAPTER TEN

'WELL, did you write the letter I requested?' John asked while they were motoring up to Bude. 'You haven't shown me a copy. I expected it to be signed, sealed and delivered by this time.'

Rebecca sat up, stiff and defiant. 'I do have other things to do, Mr Barrie.' She spoke admonishingly. 'Such as important exams to study for, besides working "one in two" at the moment, which means a hundred-and-thirty-six-hour week.' And then, anticipating contradiction, she hastily qualified that statement with, 'Yes, I know I'm *contracted* to work eighty-eight hours a week, but that's a bit different from one hundred and thirty-six.'

'Um—forty-eight hours, if my arithmetic is right.' John sighed. 'I can see it's to be one of those statistics-type conversations. I should have come prepared, but being an optimist I had thought we'd discuss more intimate matters, such as what you feel for me and what I feel for you. Wouldn't that be more interesting? The trouble is, no matter what I say, you always answer so abruptly, Rebecca. The way you called me "Mr Barrie", for instance—if anything could kill a romantic approach, that would. Why can't you call me John? Have I offended you in some way? Is that it? You know, you're a very prickly person at times.'

'*You* aren't exactly the easiest person in the world!' Rebecca retorted.

'There you go again. I don't think I've ever come across anyone more disturbingly frank than you,' he returned with either a snort or a chuckle, Rebecca couldn't decide which. 'You're certainly adept at deflating a man's ego; I'd award you an Oscar for your talent in that respect.'

'Perhaps it's the only way I can come to terms with all the criticisms I have thrown at me when in theatre,' she suggested, hoping he would take the hint and go easier on her in future.

'*Touché*!' he declared, adding a moment later, 'Well, are you going to see to the letter?'

'No,' she said unyieldingly.

'Why not?' his voice was brittle. 'Don't you agree that the medical staff need to band together if we're to get Ward Eight opened again and have no further closures in the hospital? I thought you cared about our patients?'

'And I thought this was to be a day out, away from work and all the pressures that go with it!' Rebecca snapped back, turning as if to study the passing countryside. Not that she was aware of anything other than the sudden distress she felt inside. Why was it, she asked herself, that whenever she and John were alone together they had to fight?

'Incompatible,' she muttered. 'That's what

we'd be if we were husband and wife. A stormy partnership!' Although why she should think of John in the role of husband bothered her.

'What's that?' he asked, equally irritable. 'I can't possibly hear you when you talk in a whisper, the engine's making too much noise.' He slowed the car to a standstill beside the grass verge and faced her. 'Look here, Rebecca,' he went on, 'there's something gnawing away at you, and I'd like to know what it is. We can't go on as if at daggers drawn, it's too ridiculous. Come out with it if you have a grievance. Are you still hankering after cousin Richard, and comparing me to him to my detriment? Is that it? Well, get this into your head—I'm *me*. I'm not Richard, and I don't want to be!' With that, he tipped her chin up and looked into her eyes.

'Please drive on,' she said coldly, remembering Selena.

'My hat!' John threw a frustrated glance up to the sky. 'If you're not just about the most irritating female in the world, I don't know who is!'

'More irritating than Selena?' She couldn't resist reminding him of her.

'What has Selena to do with us?' he stormed.

Shocked by his lack of conscience, Rebecca averted her head, scared that he might see the yearning and the wanting and apply them to himself, whereas of course it was Richard she ached to be with. 'Can't we drive on and join the others, *please*?' she almost begged.

'Oh, all right,' he said in a defeated voice.

They were the last to arrive at the agreed meeting place, north of Bude.

'Ah, Dr Shaw and Mr Barrie,' Anne greeted them. 'We feared we had lost you!' The rising hope in her eyes dimmed as she noted their unhappy faces. 'I'm no good as a matchmaker,' she said in an aside to her husband, shrugging defeatedly. 'I think they've quarrelled.'

'Serves you right for meddling,' Ted replied, but not without a certain fond tolerance.

'Oh, well,' Anne sighed resignedly, 'maybe we'd better invite Rebecca to come along with us on the trail.'

But Rebecca made it clear she wanted to be on her own, so Anne made no attempt to insist. 'But please keep within sight of some of us, though, won't you?' she pleaded. 'Who knows what peculiar characters lurk about on the cliffs and down in the valley? It's not safe for a girl to be seen to be on her own in such isolated places—well, not for *any* female, come to that.'

'I'll take care.' Rebecca smiled in reassurance, then walked off towards the little brook which flowed into the sea at Duckpool. The weather was fine. Dragonflies and damselflies skimmed over the water, reflecting light from their gauzy greeny-blue wings. Water lapped soothingly against rocks and stones. Tiny goldcrests and long-tailed tits flitted through the sunshine.

Rebecca stood still, drinking in all the beauty around, the early rhododendrons towering above multi-coloured wild flowers, the golden gorse lining the path she was on, the waving fronds of ferns. A squirrel ran across her path and busied itself, frantically digging through a carpet of leaf-mould, seeking the nuts buried the previous autumn.

Not moving an inch for fear of disturbing it, she was rewarded by a glimpse of a tiny harvest mouse which, even as she watched, made a comical effort at turning a somersault in an effort to avoid her foot. Laughing, she walked on. Her hair was blowing in the breeze, adding to the sense of freedom she was enjoying. Freedom from hospital corridors with their necessary disinfectant and chemical odours, freedom from the pain of seeing patients suffer, freedom from the stresses and strains of caring for them . . . and freedom from a certain difficult registrar.

Following the gurgling stream and listening to a willow-warbler singing its heart out above her, Rebecca felt like singing a song of praise herself to give thanks for all the natural beauty surrounding her.

Then, thinking the other side of the stream even more inviting, she did a balancing act across a tree-trunk bridging the water, not realising she was heading away from the nature trail she was supposed to be following.

Time had ceased to exist for her. She had left her watch in the pocket of her white coat, where she had put it the previous day before scrubbing up ready to operate.

Conscious of a growing hunger, she knew it must be way past lunchtime, but being well used to going long hours without food she was not particularly bothered. Taking off her shoes, she paddled in the stream, rolling up the legs of her jeans, but getting them pretty well soaked just the same.

Not that she minded. She was free—free to do as she liked! It was a wonderful feeling. All her cares dropped from her.

Then suddenly the atmosphere changed. An ethereal wreath of mist swept across her path. She turned, meaning to retrace her steps, but found the mist thickening behind her even more than in front. A sea mist drifting up the valley, insidiously invading the woods around her. Bird-song was silenced. The quietness was uncanny.

Not knowing how far she had walked, she feared she was going around in circles. The damp mist cooled her wet jeans, sending cold shivers up her legs. She was cold and uncomfortable. Worries crowded in on her again. The last thing she had wanted was to spoil everyone's day, she told herself miserably, yet she was probably doing just that. Anne, for one, would be worried stiff, looking for her.

Daylight began to fade. Leaves rustled, twigs snapped, firing her imagination. In the loneliness of her immediate environment, she became quite scared.

Finally she had to accept that she was completely lost, with no idea whether to go forward or back along the path she could only distinguish for a few yards either side. She started to pray for help.

Before saying more than a word or two, however, she heard a voice . . . the voice that stirred her above all others. John Barrie was calling her name.

Relieved beyond measure, she shouted back, and kept up the guiding calls until he found her.

Her hair was damp and lank with mist, but he rested his cheek on it just as once before, holding her in his arms as if he would never let her go. She couldn't see his face, or judge what he was feeling. The world was growing dark. Trees through which the sun had been dappling the ground were now like black guipure lace silhouetted against the sky, the mist lying low, obliterating only their trunks.

All Rebecca's fears disappeared, too. She was safe from harm, home where she belonged. She raised her face to meet John's kiss.

For a long moment neither of them moved. Love was in the air. Rebecca's arms were around John's neck, her hands on his head drawing it ever closer.

'John,' she murmured, 'oh, John!' with never a thought of Richard crossing her mind.

'Do you love me, Rebecca?' John murmured between kisses. 'Tell me you love me. I've been in torment, thinking I'd lost you!' He drew her closer, held her so tightly that she could hardly breathe.

Feeling loved, she rejoiced. Then, like a cloud shutting out the sun, a shadow fell across her joy. She remembered Selena again.

Pushing John away from her, she burst into tears.

Misunderstanding, he dropped his arms to his side for a moment, then, with a mere brotherly gesture, put one arm around her shoulders. 'You're overwrought,' he said quietly. 'I shouldn't have taken advantage of your distress. Obviously it was Richard you wanted. Anyway, let's get back to the others. They were all worrying about you.'

With John supporting her as best he could, together they began the climb back up the valley towards the car park.

Rebecca was unaware of what happened next until she found herself in the car again and heading towards the hospital.

'You fainted,' John explained in response to her questioning. 'Lack of food, probably. We were being floodlit by the headlamps of all the cars to help guide us up the valley, when suddenly you passed out. I had to carry you the rest of the way.'

'And we're going home?' Rebecca passed a hand over her forehead in an attempt to stimulate her memory.

'If home means the hospital. Rest now, take things quietly,' John said, his hand covering hers in a sympathetic gesture.

Another stolen moment of happiness, Rebecca

thought, loving the comfort of his touch. Yet, what right had she to gain such pleasure and solace from someone else's husband or husband-to-be? Feeling miserable and guilty, she forgot for the moment that it was Richard she was supposed to be in love with, not John. Things were getting very complicated.

John was pulling up in the forecourt of a public house. 'We could get some bar food here,' he suggested. 'You need to eat.'

'No, no, not here, I'm much too untidy.' She sank back in her seat as if to hide from public gaze. 'Let's go straight to my flat.'

They opened a tin of soup when they got there, and sat in the kitchen without bothering to do more than rest the bowls of soup on the working surface. One slice of brown bread each, all they could find, completed the frugal meal, but it was a companionable one, Rebecca returning to something like her bright self.

Afterwards, when about to leave, John mentioned a Mrs Newlyn, one of the elderly patients who had been on the surgical ward. 'You must remember her,' he reminded Rebecca. 'She came in for a laparotomy, but it wasn't needed, there was obviously nothing wrong with her. All the same, she insisted on giving you the credit, and simply because she prefers female doctors!'

'It *was* funny, wasn't it? She was so sure I'd cured her, yet I hadn't had to do a thing!'

'Well, she's longing to see you again. Keeps asking if you'll visit her. I call in on her occasionally. She lives in Helston.'

Helston, noted Rebecca. Near Culdrose. So, he's been going down to see Selena. She was immediately ashamed of the jealousy she had felt, realising it was only right and proper that he should visit the girl . . . all the same, the knowledge hurt.

John interrupted her unhappy thoughts. He was suggesting she should drive down with him to Helston to see the Furry Dance, and combine that with a brief visit to Mrs Newlyn.

'Well, I've always wanted to see what happens on the famous Flora Day,' Rebecca replied, sorely tempted to go with him. 'And it would be nice to see Mrs Newlyn again, she was quite a dear.'

'Right then,' John said briskly. 'May the eighth it is. Arrange to take the day off.' Then, before she could demur, he walked to her front door, preparing to let himself out.

Her conscience pricking her, Rebecca followed him into her tiny hall. 'Perhaps Selena would like to join us there,' she suggested—not very enthusiastically, but simply because she thought she should.

He turned, a frown of irritation crossing his face. 'Don't keep throwing Selena up at me,' he said abruptly. 'It spoils everything!'

Just what did he mean by that? Rebecca asked herself after he had gone. Was he double-dealing in some way, playing one girl off against the other? But no, he wouldn't do anything so

discreditable. Could it be that his relationship
with Selena was falling apart? And was *she*
responsible in some way? She'd been very careful
not to intervene, hadn't she? Well, until the
events of the day had overtaken her . . .

She allowed herself to remember her response
to John's kisses. An involuntary response
stimulated by her intense relief at being found.
That was all it was, she assured herself.
Nevertheless, she felt culpable again, knowing in
her heart that she had experienced ecstasy for the
first time in her life, and would treasure those
stolen moments as long as she lived.

She marked a ring around May the eighth on
her calendar, then, spurring herself on to study,
opened a large volume on surgical pathology.
With the Final Fellowship of the Royal College
of Surgeons exam looming high on her horizon,
she knew there was no time to spare for day-
dreaming. Unless she passed the Final she would
never be able to become a consultant. Rebecca
was too ambitious not to climb to the top of the
tree. Besides, she felt she had the necessary
surgical skill, and was determined not to waste
the gift she had been given in that direction.

'Guide me, dear Lord, help me heal your sick,'
was her favourite prayer, and she knew she would
be expected to make much of the effort herself,
instead of leaving it all to Him, so she worked
hard and studied hard.

May the eighth provided a problem in two
directions. It would not only mean losing a day's

learning and studying, but she wasn't at all sure she would be doing the right thing in accompanying John. Her conscience was already heavily taxed, so, in spite of the almost irresistible temptation, she decided not to usurp Selena's place yet again.

'Of course you're coming,' John said in his masterful way when she told him of her decision not to go to Helston, giving the need to study as her excuse. 'You won't get another chance to see the Furry Dance. It takes place only once a year—you might be off to another hospital when your present contract ends, and it won't be in Cornwall. Double your study time when you return; we'll come back early.'

'The nursing staff are talking about hiring a coach to take all off-duty personnel,' Rebecca suggested next. 'Perhaps I ought to go with them.'

'Nonsense!' John vetoed the idea immediately. 'You want to get back early, and the others will stop off on the way back to celebrate the day's outing, possibly staying out until the early hours, whereas I can bring you straight back.'

His argument seemed to make sense, so she left the arrangements as they were and went to the sisters' office to tell Anne her plans.

'What happened to you yesterday?' Anne asked afterwards. 'Did you get lost in Coombe Valley? I haven't had a chance to ask Mr Barrie.'

'Completely lost.' Rebecca pulled a face. 'My own fault entirely, I should have had more faith

and trust, but instead I panicked when I found
myself enveloped in mist again, like that time
when I was driving back from Culdrose. There
was no visibility at all to speak of.'

'I know Mr Barrie was very concerned about
you—he rushed down into the valley as soon as
you were reported missing. Y'know, I think you
mean quite a lot to him.'

Rebecca made no comment, aware that Anne
knew nothing about his secret marriage.

'Anyway,' Anne chatted on, 'there's some
excitement brewing. Kiran's arrived from India
and we're all longing to know what Dr Patel
thinks of him. She's promised to bring him on
the coach we've booked for Helston. It's a pity
you won't be with us.'

'I have to get back early,' Rebecca said, but as
she spoke her colour rose and, looking at her,
Anne nodded knowingly.

'I suppose Mr Barrie is taking you?' She
smiled. 'I like a good romance!'

'It's merely for my convenience,' Rebecca put
in hastily. 'He knows I want to be able to get in
some study so he's bringing me back early.'

'Oh, is that it?' Anne raised her eyebrows, her
expression remaining unconvinced.

'What's happened to Dr Dunn?' Rebecca
asked, to change the subject before it could
become even more embarrassing.

'No one knows. At least, I expect Admin has a
good idea, but if so they're keeping it to
themselves. He was in an awful mood that last

day he was here, wasn't he? Maybe he's sick or something.'

'I don't think there was anything wrong with him other than an indefatigable thirst for alcohol,' Rebecca commented. 'Otherwise he could be quite nice, when it pleased him to make the effort. If only he didn't drink so much—it's ruining him! Such an awful waste of a good anaesthetist!'

'Have you heard any more about the ward closure?' Anne asked.

Rebecca looked a little awkward, remembering John's anger over the unwritten letter. 'Not yet,' she said, 'but I'm leaving the matter to the seniors now. Their protest will carry more weight than that of junior doctors.'

'Well, it's a good let-out,' said Anne astutely, 'and you did do your bit.'

'That's what I think. Oh, well, back to work!'

CHAPTER ELEVEN

MAY the eighth dawned warm and sunny, and Rebecca set off to Helston with John, but without the misgivings she had expected to have. He had not bothered her again outside work, so she felt more secure, taking it for granted that he realised the emotive scene down in Coombe Valley had resulted purely and simply from accumulated stress on both their parts.

Their conversation on the way down was specifically about medical matters and patients, and kept them engrossed until they reached Helston, where John drew up outside a small terrace-house.

Mrs Newlyn answered the ringing of her doorbell, a wide smile of welcome on her face. 'I remember you,' she said to Rebecca. 'If it hadn't been for your great skill in surgery, I'd never have survived!'

Trying to keep a serious face, in spite of John's amused expression, Rebecca turned her attention to the dress Mrs Newlyn had laid out ready to show her, the one she had worn to Furry Dances in her youth. Brightly coloured once, it had become a faded print, but one could still distinguish the famous sprigged pattern, which

169

was the only acceptable one in those days, according to Mrs Newlyn.

'Fabric sold for a Furry gown wouldn't have any more taken from its bale until after Flora Day,' she stressed. 'It would have been quite unthinkable for two dancers to wear dresses made from the same roll of material. Identical gowns were quite *infra dig* in those days. You know what I mean?'

Tea and saffron cake followed the viewing of the treasured gown. Then John and Rebecca left to see the dance beginning at the Guildhall and continuing through the gaily decorated streets, led by Helston's town band. The music accompanying the dance, although so well-known, had never been written down, but had simply been passed on from bandmaster to bandmaster, or so Mrs Newlyn had informed Rebecca.

Dancing had begun as early as seven in the morning—townsfolk who would be spending the rest of the day serving the needs of the crowds having their own 'Faddy' then.

'I heard someone say that participation in these later dances is by invitation only,' Rebecca said, her feet tapping to the catchy music as she watched the dancers spiralling rhythmically in and out of homes and gardens. 'I wish I could join in,' she added wistfully.

'Now, don't be getting ideas.' John sounded alarmed. 'I'm no dancer. In any case, the leaders have to have been born in Helston, which lets me out!'

'You take it for granted you'd be chosen as a leader?'

'Naturally, dancer or no dancer. What else would you expect?' He smiled as he spoke, however, then went on to remark, 'There was a time when anyone found at work here on Flora Day was carried shoulder-high to the River Cober and made to jump over Pengellow Water. Not a nice thing to have to do, considering it's a bottomless pool! I wonder how doctors got on? Did they have to leave the sick to suffer unattended for the day?'

'It's a good thing times have changed.' Rebecca shivered at the thought of the duckings. 'What would you have done? Refused to give people operations, even if emergencies cropped up?'

'Maybe operations were few and far between in those days. One thing's certain, there wouldn't have been any female surgeons, so you'd have been safe sitting at home knitting—or spinning—and perhaps joining those lovely girls in their white dresses, with flowers in your hair and carrying a floral half-hoop above your head, once a year on Flora Day. Mind you, no girl could have competed with you—you're quite dramatically beautiful when your hair outshines the sun, as now.'

Rebecca blushed self-consciously. 'Have you noticed how even the police have buttonholes of sprigs of lily of the valley?' she put in quickly, to make him look anywhere but at her, his gaze being too intense for her comfort. Then, because she thought she should, she mentioned Selena again. 'Shouldn't you be meeting her somewhere?' she asked pointedly.

'Whatever for?' His mood changed, annoyance taking over.

Rebecca hesitated, sorry to have had to spoil things for him by talking realities. 'I—I just thought you'd be wanting to see some of your Culdrose friends . . .' She stumbled over her words, feeling awkward, and fearing she was inviting his anger again.

'Selena has nothing to do with Culdrose, she just likes to hang around there. Not that the men encourage her. I didn't either,' he declared rather crossly.

She wouldn't need encouragement, Rebecca wanted to say, but stopped herself in time. 'Shall we go to the coach park and see if the others have arrived?' she suggested mildly instead.

'A meal first.' John led the way to a small restaurant. 'I'm in no hurry to get caught up in a crowd again,' he added curtly. Fortunately the excellent lunch helped to put him into a better temper, and afterwards, upon going outside, they met Seema, who introduced them to her fiancé, Kiran Shah, who was every bit as likeable as Seema had hoped. The two of them appeared to be very well-matched and, envying them their obvious happiness, Rebecca sighed.

Marriage was in the air, it seemed to her. Romance was blossoming everywhere, in the streets, in the parks, in the gaiety of the dancing couples. All that was needed was for Richard to join her, then she, too, could make happy plans for the future.

Walking along the narrow raised pathway outside the restaurant after leaving Seema and Kiran, John drew back suddenly, as if wishing to change direction. 'See who's coming towards us?' he muttered. 'I think you must have wished her up!'

'Hi!' said Selena. 'Have you seen Geoffrey anywhere?' Serious-faced, she continued to gaze over the heads of the passing throng on the pavement below, making no attempt to kiss John, much to Rebecca's relief. 'He was meant to partner me in the Gentry Dance,' Selena added absently.

'Is that the dance in which men wear silk hats and frock-coats, and the girls are in pretty dresses and flower-decked bonnets?' Rebecca asked.

'Maybe he wasn't able to get away.' Selena remained vague, not attempting to answer.

'Get away from where?' John asked sharply, to get her to take notice.

'From the private clinic he's attending, of course.'

'Why, what's wrong with him?' Rebecca and John asked as one.

'He's been told he drinks too much, so he's getting help to stop. Taken some holiday leave. I wonder where he's got to? Maybe further down Helston Ley? Anyway, I'll look. He'll be disappointed if he can't find me. See you!'

'You don't mind?' Rebecca asked John afterwards, imagining him suffering.

'Mind?' He almost laughed. 'Mind because she's off my back and chasing after Geoffrey instead?'

'You're very callous—most men would be up in arms about their girls running after someone else!' There, thought Rebecca, now I've let the cat out of the bag! She told herself she didn't care, she was so disillusioned. John had commanded respect in the hospital, but he certainly did nothing to deserve any when outside! The idea of it, letting his wife chase around after Geoffrey . . . wife, fiancée or girlfriend, what difference did it make?

'Look,' he interrupted her thoughts, 'I don't know what bee you have in your bonnet, Rebecca, but if you're trying to goad me into admitting some secret passion for Selena, then you'll never succeed. I'd have thought you'd give me credit for making a better choice than Selena . . . of all people, *Selena*!'

His face was grim again, his eyes dark and angry.

'I was told that you and she were secretly married, or about to be.'

'Married?' His astonishment was such that his voice boomed, and heads turned. 'Who on earth told you that?'

'Geoffrey,' she said in a low tone, meant to quieten him down.

'And you believed him? You didn't stop to think that perhaps he had some axe to grind and was trying to come between us?'

'He had no need to bother, you seem to forget that it's *Richard* I'm planning to marry, not you!' Rebecca's temper was rising too, and although the sun was still shining and the dancing continuing it seemed to her that the joy had gone out of everything. And it was all John's fault!

In an uncomfortable silence they collected the car from outside Mrs Newlyn's house and drove back to the hospital, Rebecca pretending to doze all the way in order to avoid the need to talk.

John dropped her off outside her flat and, although he waited until she was safely inside, he moved off without saying more than a curt goodnight.

After a restless few hours' sleep Rebecca got up, made herself a cup of tea, then tried to apply her mind to her books. It was an impossible task, her thoughts were in such an unhappy tangle, so, needing to be more active while so restless inside, she tidied her flat, cleared up the kitchen and went over to the hospital, wanting to be early for John's ward round.

It would have been nice had he greeted her, she thought, but instead he immediately tossed the most gruelling medical questions her way, taking on the role of tutor again, discarding that of friend.

They worked together in theatre afterwards, but very much as part of a team, keeping to formalities and never slipping back into companionship. Rebecca was surprised how much she missed their former comparative closeness, even if it had had its unpleasant, even explosive, connotations at times.

They had so little to do with one another during the next few days that she was left wondering why he bothered when he sought her out to tell her he would be going away for a couple of days, although it turned out that all he really wanted was to inform her about the possible difficulties which might arise in the appendicectomy he had to leave for her to see to. 'You're experienced enough and capable enough to cope well,' he had the grace to say, adding that he wanted her to take particular care over this special patient of his.

'Why, who is it?' she asked.

'Veronica Main.'

'The young mother who had to have part of her brain removed after that near fatal road accident? But wouldn't a general anaesthetic put her in danger?'

'Not if our consultant anaesthetist handles it. I wouldn't risk her with anyone junior to him.'

'But you'll be happy about me doing the operation?'

'Of course. Appendicectomies are your speciality, aren't they?' he said quite seriously. 'And don't worry about it. Veronica has made a wonderful recovery, with no loss of any faculties. Her children have helped enormously. She's determined to get back to them as quickly as possible. It's a pity about the appendicitis, but it doesn't really affect anything. She'll just stay a little longer in the neurosurgical ward, that's all.'

'It's a pity they can't do the appendicectomy themselves,' Rebecca said ruefully.

'You don't mean that—you know you'd make a better job of it.'

A warm glow entered Rebecca's heart once again, thawing the ice that had been building up. John still had confidence in her ability as surgeon. That was wonderful to know.

Veronica Main came through the operation very well, with no bad after-effects, much to Rebecca's relief. She had been very anxious about her, and quite nervous about doing the operation, but when she found Veronica sitting up the next day, smiling, and enjoying her lunch, she could have danced her way around the hospital.

Instead she took John's clinic and got on with her work, determined to leave no backlog for him to catch up with on his return. She was glad to have the extra work. Life seemed colourless without him around. She found herself almost counting the hours until he was due back, which rather amazed her. She had expected to be relaxed and relieved with him away.

As if to cheer her up, however, the four-year-old boy whose appendix she had removed came in with his mother, and presented her with a posy of flowers from his own garden, accompanying it with a spontaneous kiss and cuddle, delighting her.

Also little Mrs Williams called in, accompanied by her favourite niece who had moved in with her, to take care of her, so that she could stay in her own home. Rebecca found herself deeply touched to have been remembered, and after her visitors had gone she tried to point out to Tim that although the job they were trying to do was exhausting, even quite horrifying at times, there were compensations.

She did her best to tell him this, but words dried up in her, so she went along to the little chapel where she could pour her heart out as emotionally as she pleased and know she would be understood, even if unable to put her feelings into words.

Coming out, she hurried back to theatre and was met by a wide-eyed Anne. 'Mr Barrie's asking for you, he's in the doctors' room,' she said. 'And what d'you think, he has his twin with him!'

'He hasn't one.' Rebecca puckered her brow.

'His brother, then, they're very alike.'

'He hasn't——' Rebecca stopped herself before she could deny the existence of a brother. What did it matter? The thing was that Anne must have seen a look-alike, which could only mean Richard!

Her heart playing tricks, her mouth drying and knees a little wobbly, she made her way along to the doctors' room, wondering all the time what she should say, how to behave . . .

She opened the door. The two men at the window turned, and, while she longed to run to the one, her heart withdrew from the other. She could see differences between the two which Anne had not appeared to notice. She hesitated. Always she had pictured her reunion with Richard as an impulsive merging together in an ardent embrace, with him holding her as if never to let her go again, while she would cling to him equally enthusiastically, with the stirrings of passion . . .

Instead, she stood hesitating, and he made no move towards her. John looked from one to the other and walked to the door. 'I'll leave you while I have a chat with Mr Hill,' he said, seeming rather awkward himself. 'You must have a lot to talk about.'

Richard broke the silence after the door closed. Walking towards Rebecca, and taking one of her hands in both of his, he said, 'It's been a long time!'

'Why haven't you kept in contact?' Rebecca asked, surprised at the sudden command she had over herself. She could have been talking to a chance acquaintance, rather than to the man she had hoped to marry.

'Why haven't *you*?' he retaliated, softening his blunt approach with a comment on the beauty of her hair, which he said was more spectacular than ever.

Ignoring the compliment, she said, 'I didn't know where you were, Richard. In any case, I thought it was your place to get in touch with me.'

He dropped her hand. 'Oh, come off it, Rebecca, you were never one to give males the prerogative over females. Your particular bugbear was chauvinism, if I remember rightly!'

How easily we could quarrel again, thought Rebecca, wondering where all the magic had gone. The anticipated thrill of being together, the excitement of reunion, the overwhelming love and desire—it was all missing. John had been right when he had accused her of living in a fool's paradise, always picturing Richard as she wanted him to be, not as he really was. She'd loved a dream, had waited three years for that dream to become reality. How stupid she had been—or was it that she was expecting too much too quickly?

'John didn't tell me he would be bringing you,' she said a little contritely, sorry because of her total lack of emotional response. 'I'm afraid it came as quite a shock.'

'I think it was meant as a surprise. We met up at a recent conference, hadn't seen each other for years until then, so arranged to meet again here. He was very insistent, and of course I wanted to see you.'

'Are you a surgeon, too?' Rebecca asked to change the subject, feeling uncomfortable because she was so unable to show the enthusiasm and pleasure she was sure he expected of her.

'A surgeon? Not me.' His lips curled in

distaste. '*I'm* no butcher!'

The way he said it roused Rebecca's anger. Normally she might have found the reference to surgery as butchery mildly amusing, having often heard surgeons quoting the simile as a joke against themselves . . . but Richard was being serious and trying to disparage the job she valued so highly.

Another awkward silence followed. Richard was studying her, a strange, calculating look in the eyes that were so like John's. A contemplating look. Was he wondering what answer she would give if he said he was now ready for marriage? Rebecca's heart sank, dreading what he might have come to say. Her breath came quickly, almost with a touch of panic. She looked to the door. Why, oh, why didn't John come back? Suddenly she needed his support so urgently that she could easily have cried out for him.

Still Richard said nothing, seemingly lost for words. The atmosphere grew tense—unbearably so, thought Rebecca, struggling against growing fears.

The door opened and John walked in, accompanied by Mr Hill, to whom Richard was introduced, but as John's cousin, not as her fiancé, much to her relief.

'Have you heard the great news?' Mr Hill turned to Rebecca. 'Admin has had a rethink. Ward Eight's to be reopened!'

'Ward Eight?' she echoed vaguely, as if never having heard of it. Then, collecting her thoughts together, she took her eyes from Richard and realised what Mr Hill had said. 'Oh, marvellous.' She tried hard to raise a smile. 'Absolutely fabulous!' she tried again to enthuse, knowing it was expected of her, although she was still rather lost in her own personal problems.

'I knew you'd be pleased. Your efforts helped us achieve our goal.' Mr Hill scrutinised her astutely, glanced shrewdly from her to John, then turned to Richard. 'Come and have a look at our geriatric unit,' he invited. 'I believe you're specialising in medicine for the elderly?'

Richard needed no second invitation. His relief was obvious as he hurried out into the corridor away from Rebecca.

'We'll meet you in the canteen for lunch at one,' John called after him, before carefully closing the door. 'I brought him along purposely,' he said, his voice and face very earnest and his hands digging deep into his trouser pockets. 'You see, Rebecca, it's become vitally important to me to find out whether or not you still wish to marry him, and I knew that after your long separation you'd need to meet him again before you could make a balanced decision. Tell me,' his blue eyes were uncertain and apprehensive, '*do* you still want to marry Richard?'

Rebecca stared down at the floor. 'Why should it be so important for you to know?' she countered.

'Because . . . oh, just because . . .' His

expression grew pained. 'Oh, my dear girl, can't you possibly give me a straight answer?'

She remained gazing at the floor, knowing that if she raised her eyes he would detect the love and desire in them and possibly misunderstand, but the next second his hands were out of his pockets and placed firmly on her shoulders, shaking them none too gently. 'Tell me, Rebecca, you *must* tell me,' he said demandingly, 'do you still want to marry Richard?'

His hands were warm and strong. The impulse to lean her head to one side and feel his touch on her skin was almost irresistible. Surely, she thought, he could feel the love her heart was pouring out to him?

She chose her words carefully. 'All this time I've been struggling to keep alive a love which existed only in my wishful thinking, stubbornly refusing to accept that what Richard and I had shared was nothing more than an immature infatuation. We'd been light-hearted companions, both of us in love with love, and mistaking that for the real thing.'

'Which is?' he asked, his hands gentle now, his voice suddenly full of tenderness.

She stood biting her lips, and trying to blink away an insistent mistiness from her eyes. 'It might sound very sentimental,' she said, in such a low voice that he had to bend his head to hear it, 'but I think that true love involves putting the welfare and happiness of someone else above anything one wants for oneself . . . and by "someone else" I mean——'

'*Me*?' John asked brightly, without the least discomposure. 'An incredible feeling, isn't it? Tears one to pieces at times! I know it well, after all, I've lived with it for years—three to be precise—but now I'm growing happier and more optimistic by the second, sure that my unfailing and extremely unselfish love is to be rewarded at long last. Rebecca, look at me!' His voice was strong and commanding again. 'Let me get this straight. You're trying to tell me that what you felt for Richard was not love, but simply infatuation?'

She nodded, her eyes shy. 'And sadly, infatuation dies,' she murmured, 'whereas real love lives forever.'

'I couldn't agree more, so now I'm free to show you this.' John produced a snapshot from his pocket with one hand, still holding her close with the other.

Rebecca stared at the photo. 'Oh, it's of a wedding—so you *are* married!' she exclaimed in some distress, pushing him away.

'No, no, no, take another look at the groom—it's Richard, not me!' John had to hold her tighter than ever then, to steady her. 'I first learned of his marriage when I returned from overseas. Now you know why I chose to come to this hospital; a little bird told me you were working here, somewhere, although I certainly didn't expect to find you doing surgery. An ethereal being like you holding your own among

giants of surgeons like me? That has come as a
shock, I admit, although not as much of a shock
as I'm experiencing now, when seeing for myself
the wealth of love in your eyes and knowing it's
for *me*—and it is, isn't it, my dearest dear?'

Rebecca had no need to answer, her loving
expression said it all for her.

'I'm sorry it was necessary to shake you out of
your fantasy,' he murmured, smoothing her
russet curls with his cheek. 'I asked Richard not
to tell you he was married. I needed to see for
myself how you'd react to meeting him while still
thinking him free to marry you. I could never
have endured being a second-best, Rebecca, nor
could I have lived with the fear hanging over me
that you were marrying me on the rebound.
Because you *are* going to marry me,' he declared
in his masterful way.

'Am I?' She leaned up against his broad chest,
her face every bit as radiant as her hair, stars of
wonder beginning to shimmer in her opaquely
green eyes. 'It's funny,' she said dreamily, 'but I
sensed a strange awkwardness between Richard
and myself when we met just now. I suppose it
was difficult for him to know what to say; he
must have been longing to at least mention his
marriage, but couldn't because of your request. I
was equally at a loss to know what to say to him,
because the moment I saw the two of you
together, I knew in my heart of hearts which one
I loved. But now, in the light of Richard's
marriage, I'll be able to talk freely to him, all

barriers removed. We can be friends. I wonder what his wife is like? Do I know her? I'm glad we're having lunch with him, there are three years of news to catch up with!'

'But for the moment you can forget him.' John pulled a surgical cap from his pocket, smiling down at her as she eyed it curiously. 'This is my treasure,' he claimed. 'I keep it with me always. You see, it once sat upon the most colourful, wonderful, coppery-auburn hair in all the world—hair that is a veritable Caribbean cocktail of shades—a Caribbean sunset, as you once told me, remember?'

Then, as if growing so impatiently hungry for her that he was unable to wait any longer, he lowered his head until his lips met hers. Rebecca closed her eyes, responding to his long, lingering kiss with every loving fibre of her being.

Finally, suddenly remembering she was supposed to be on duty, she drew away from him to glance at her watch. 'I'm due in theatre!' she gasped, making for the door a little unsteadily. There she turned, holding on to the doorpost for support, her face alive with the old impish sparkle which had been missing for so long.

'I hope you realise that Ward Eight's being reopened even *without* the help of that follow-up letter I was almost pressurised into writing.' She raised her eyebrows, adding a smug, 'I knew it wouldn't be necessary!'

'"Almost" is the operative word,' John said in his most arrogant manner. 'Now run along to theatre, young lady. I'll follow on. Being officially on leave still, I'll have time to sit and criticise—you'll like that, won't you?' Then, noticing the face she pulled, he added a little less confidently, 'But tell me, Rebecca, you don't find me *too* awkward, do you?'

'Oh, no, Dr Difficult,' she replied, tongue in cheek, before escaping out into the corridor.

Hello!

As a reader, you may not have thought about trying to write a book yourself, but if you have, and you have a particular interest in medicine, then now is your chance.

We are specifically looking for new writers to join our established team of authors who write Medical Romances. Guidelines are available for this list, and we would be happy to send them to you.

Please mark the outside of your envelope 'Medical' to help speed our response, and we would be most grateful if you could include a stamped self-addressed envelope, size approximately $9\frac{1}{4}''$ x $4\frac{3}{4}''$, sent to the address below.

We look forward to hearing from you.

Editorial Department,
Mills & Boon Limited,
Eton House,
18-24 Paradise Road,
Richmond, Surrey,
TW9 1SR.

THE IDEAL TONIC

Over the past year, we have listened carefully to readers' comments, and so, in August, Mills & Boon are launching a *new look* Doctor-Nurse series – MEDICAL ROMANCES.

There will still be three books every month from a wide selection of your favourite authors. As a special bonus, the three books in August will have a special offer price of **ONLY** 99p each.

So don't miss out on this chance to get a real insight into the fast-moving and varied world of modern medicine, which gives such a unique background to drama, emotions – and romance!

FRUIT SALAD WORDSEARCH
COMPETITION!

How would you like a years supply of Mills & Boon Romances ABSOLUTELY FREE? Well, you can win them! All you have to do is complete the word puzzle below and send it in to us by Dec. 31st. 1989. The first 5 correct entries picked out of the bag after that date will win **a years supply of Mills & Boon Romances** (*ten books every month - worth £162*) What could be easier?

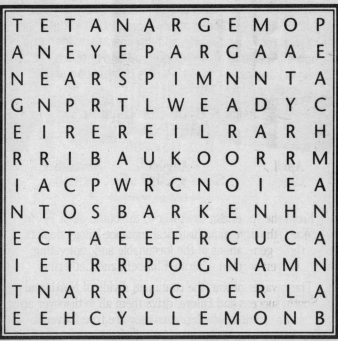

```
T E T A N A R G E M O P
A N E Y E P A R G A A E
N E A R S P I M N N T A
G N P R T L W E A D Y C
E I R E R E I L R A R H
R R I B A U K O O R R M
I A C P W R C N O I E A
N T O S B A R K E N H N
E C T A E E F R C U C A
I E T R R P O G N A M N
T N A R R U C D E R L A
E E H C Y L L E M O N B
```

RASPBERRY	ORANGE	LYCHEE
REDCURRANT	MANGO	CHERRY
BANANA	LEMON	KIWI
TANGERINE	APRICOT	GRAPE
STRAWBERRY	PEACH	PEAR
POMEGRANATE	MANDARIN	APPLE
BLACKCURRANT	NECTARINE	MELON

PLEASE TURN OVER FOR DETAILS ON HOW TO ENTER

HOW TO ENTER

All the words listed overleaf, below the word puzzle, are hidden in the grid. You can find them by reading the letters forward, backwards, up or down, or diagonally. When you find a word, circle it or put a line through it, the remaining letters (which you can read from left to right, from the top of the puzzle through to the bottom) will spell a secret message.

After you have filled in all the words, don't forget to fill in your name and address in the space provided and pop this page in an envelope (you don't need a stamp) and post it today. Hurry - competition ends December 31st. 1989.

Mills & Boon Competition,
FREEPOST,
P.O. Box 236,
Croydon,
Surrey. CR9 9EL

Only one entry per household

Secret Message _____

_____

Name _____

Address _____

_____

_____

_____ Postcode _____

You may be mailed as a result of entering this competition
Please tick the box if you are a Reader Service subscriber ☐

COMP7